SOULMATE

1ST BOOK OF THE SERIES

TANUSHKA RAHA. RAI
(AUTHOR NAME)

"To everyone whose sacrifice goes unnoticed"

Contents

Contents

FOREWORD

Soulmate, often described as the romantic partner or the love of your life. But it's actual meaning goes much deeper than that. It is a person with whom you share a deep, natural and spiritual connection. The relationships that feel easy, as if you've known each other forever. They help you grow and evolve. It includes, lovers, friends, families, classmates and who knows, maybe many other .

Preface

That night, under the sacred vows and burning flames, **Tara became Queen of a man who would never know the truth.**

As Nayna sailed away into the unknown, Tara lowered her veil, hiding the quiet triumph in her eyes.

No man, not even a king, could take away her sister's freedom.

Acknowledgements

This is the 1st book I am publishing on my own without any help, so if I make any mistakes, I apologise for that. I want to thank all of my supporters who encouraged me in this whole journey. Specially my parents and one particular tution teacher. Thanks to one of my close friends to help me make the cover of this book .And yes, how can I forget my two friends who were almost simping over the book each day. Thankyou so much.

If you want to check more of my work, please follow @bibilophile_princess on Instagram.

Trigger Warning

Disclaimer

This is a work of fiction, abuses and crimes shown in this story
are not encouraged by the author.

Blood
Emotional neglect
Child abuse
Child marriage
Terrorist
Polygamy
Heart break
Many more.

Playlists

Dhoop (Shreya Ghoshal, Siddharth, Garima)
Albela Sajan (Shashi Suman, Kunal Pandit, Prithvi)
AJ Ibaadat (Javed Bashir, Shadab Faridi, Altamash)
Ghar More Pardesiya (Pritam, Shreya Ghoshal)
Ek Dil Ek Jaan (Shivam Pathak, A.M. Turaz)
Deewani Mastani (Shreya Ghoshal)
Jashn-E- Bahaaraa (A.R. Rahman, Javed Ali)
Dheeme Dheeme (Shreya Ghoshal, Ram Sampath)

I

"How dare you?!"

The furious voice of a King,the ruler of a vast and formidable kingdom, Barandesh. Thundered through the grand chamber. His dark eyes burned with dissatisfaction as he glared at the aging King Darshan, who sat before him, his face lined with worry.

"King Darshan, if you refuse to wed your daughter to me, then prepare for war!" Harshat's rage was unsettling, his demand absolute.

"But King Harshat—" king Darshan began, his voice laced with desperation, his hands instinctively tightening around the folds of his robe, hoping to find comfort.

"No buts!" Harshat cut him off, his fury unyielding. "This is my only condition. I expect your answer soon!"

With that, the young and formidable king stormed out of the chamber, leaving behind an air thick with tension. The heavy wooden doors slammed shut, their echo lingering in the silence that followed.

King Darshan exhaled shakily, his heart weighed down by a decision no father should have to make.

꙰

Nayna—the only daughter of King Darshan and Queen Rukmini—was the jewel of their kingdom, the light of their lives.

She was not just a princess, but a spirited young girl, family oriented and full of mischief. The palace walls had often witnessed her laughter, ringing through the corridors like music. Her greatest joy, however, was her cousin, Tara.

Though they were not sisters by blood, their bond was unbreakable. The palace had long since stopped calling them by separate names, instead, their names flowed together as one—Nayantara.

Born three years before Nayna, Tara had always taken on the role of an elder sister, watching over her with unwavering love and care. They had spent their childhood sneaking out into the bustling marketplace in disguise, much to the horror of their caretakers, only to return hours later, giggling at their own little adventure.

But Tara's life had not been as fortunate as Nayna's.

Her parents—her mother, sister of Queen Rukmini, and her father, a commoner—had met a tragic end. The loss left Tara orphaned, but she did not remain alone for long. The king and queen had taken her in without hesitation, raising her as their own. She was not just a niece; she was a princess in her own right.

The two sisters had flourished under the love of their family, wrapped in the comfort of a world that felt safe.

But safety is a fragile thing.

The arrival of King Harshat shattered that peace.

He had come to see Nayna, lured by whispers of her unparalleled beauty. But his intentions were far from noble. He was a man who collected wives like trophies, a ruler whose name instilled fear rather than admiration.

When he proposed marriage, King Darshan refused without hesitation. He knew Harshat's nature well, knew that his daughter's life would be reduced to nothing more than a decorative piece in his grand court—a mere addition to his countless queens.

But Harshat did not take rejection lightly.

He issued an ultimatum: either his daughter would be his bride, or Nazabgar would face war.

Now, King Darshan stood at the turn of an impossible choice.

On one side was his daughter—the child he had sworn to protect, the soul he could not bear to see in chains.

On the other was his kingdom—a land of peace, a people who had never known the horrors of war. The other child he was bound to protect as their king.

Nazabgar was not a land of warriors. It was a kingdom that thrived on harmony, where swords were sheathed more often than they were drawn. Against Harshat's mighty army, they stood no chance.

His heart ached, torn between his duty as a king and his love as a father.

What path could he take where he did not lose everything?

II

King Darshan paced in his bed chamber, his face etched with worry, his heart weighed down by an impossible dilemma.

"What will I do, Rukmini?!" he cried, his voice heavy with anguish. "How can I hand over my daughter to that tyrant just to protect the kingdom? But if I refuse... if I put her first, I will be failing my people—people who trust me as their king! How can I choose between my daughter and my duty?"

His voice trembled as he sat on the edge of the bed, defeated.

Queen Rukmini, though equally distraught, remained composed. She reached for his hand, her touch gentle yet firm.

"Maharaj," she said softly, "why don't we discuss this with our daughters? They are not children anymore. They are wise, and they must learn to face the burdens of royalty. Perhaps they will see a path we cannot."

Darshan sighed deeply. He had hoped to shelter his daughters from such cruel realities a little longer. To him, they were still the mischievous little girls who ran through the palace gardens, laughing under the sun. How could he place such a weight upon their young shoulders?

But Rukmini was right. The world would not spare them from hardship, and in a kingdom ruled by men, their battles would always be harder.

As he wrestled with his thoughts, he did not realize—his daughters were already listening.

From behind the heavy curtains, Nayna and Tara stood still, their hearts pounding as they absorbed every word.

&

"Baba."

Darshan turned sharply at the sound of his daughter's voice. Nayna and Tara stepped forward, their expressions unreadable.

"I didn't mean to overhear," Nayna admitted, her hands clutching a small bundle of flowers she and Tara had picked in the garden. "But I heard everything."

Darshan's face fell. He cursed this torment, but now, his daughter was standing before him, aware of the storm looming over them.

"Putri..." His voice wavered. "Never did I imagine I would have to face such a day. I don't know what to do."

Nayna took a step closer. Then, with a steady breath, she placed the flowers in an empty vase and spoke the words that sent a jolt through the room.

"Accept the proposal, Baba. I will marry King Harshat."

Silence.....

The air grew thick with shock.

"No!!" Queen Rukmini was the first to react. Her voice was strong, but her hands trembled as she gripped her daughter's shoulders. "I will never allow you to marry that vile man!"

"Mata," Nayna's voice was unwavering, though her eyes shone with sadness. "There is no other choice. I have lived my whole life with the privileges of a princess. If I have taken from this kingdom, then I must give back. This is my responsibility."

These were the words they had been raised with. A royal's duty was not just to rule—it was to sacrifice and protect when needed.

Her words rang with the weight of truth, and none could argue against them. The silence stretched long.

Except for Tara.

Unlike the others, she had not spoken a word. She stood eerily still, her eyes dark with thought.

Then, she broke her silence.

"Yes, Maharaj, Maharani," Tara said, her voice calm and deliberate. "Nayna is right. She is the princess. This is her duty."

Darshan turned to her, searching her face for hesitation. There was none.

"But—"

"No buts, Maharaj," Tara interrupted gently. She stepped forward, placing a reassuring hand on his. "You raised me as your own daughter, didn't you? Then trust me. I will never let my sister be unhappy."

There was something final in her words, something neither the king nor queen could challenge.

Darshan exhaled shakily. He looked at his daughters—his little girls who had grown too fast.

"Fine," he whispered at last. "You are both mature enough to make your own decisions."

But his heart felt as if it were bleeding.

જી

That night, Nayna sat in her room, her fingers absentmindedly tracing the embroidery of her attire.

Tara entered quietly, her presence grounding as always.

"Nayna," she teased, a small smile tugging at her lips. "Why do you look so sad? Didn't you say you were ready for marriage?"

Nayna huffed, throwing a pillow at her. "Di, don't mock me! You know this isn't a real wedding. That man—he collects wives like ornaments. He already has over twenty. I will just be another forgotten queen behind stone walls."

Tara looked at her for a long moment, memories flashing in her mind. Of stolen adventures, of whispered dreams, of two girls who had always been each other's strength.

"Don't you remember what I said?" Tara whispered, pulling Nayna into a tight embrace. "I will never let my sister be unhappy."

Nayna pulled back slightly, frowning. "What do you mean...?"

Both of them lied down on the bed.

Tara only smiled. "Just sleep." She gently covered Nayna's eyes with her hand.

☙

The wedding day arrived. The palace bustled with preparations, but behind closed doors, another fate was unfolding.

In Nayna's chamber, Tara stood before her, her expression solid.

"Change into this." She thrust a bundle of simple, worn clothing into Nayna's hands.

Nayna blinked in confusion. "But Di, these are maidservant's clothes. Why—?"

"No questions," Tara cut her off. "Just trust me."

Something in Tara's urgency made Nayna obey. She slipped into the rough fabric, her heartbeat quickening.

Tara moved swiftly, gathering Nayna's bridal attire and draping it over herself. The moment she lifted the heavy veil over her face, the truth hit Nayna like a crashing wave.

"Di... what are you doing?" She asked cautiously.

Tara turned to her, eyes filled with fierce love.

"Nayna, listen to me very carefully. Take the hidden passage behind this room. It will lead you to the small forest behind the castle. By the first tree, you will find a bundle of supplies—food, clothes, money. Take them and go to the harbor. There is a ship waiting. Leave this country."

Nayna felt her breath hitch. "What?! No! If I leave, who will—?"

"I will marry Harshat." Tara's voice was resolute. "I am also Maharaj's daughter. After my parents died, you became my only family. This is my choice."

"But Di—" Nayna's voice cracked. "You don't know him. You don't understand what you're sacrificing—"

"And he doesn't know me." Tara smiled, a knowing glint in her eyes. Trying to comfort her sister.

Tears welled in Nayna's eyes. "Di, I can't let you do this—"

"If you stay, I swear I will end my life." Tara's voice dropped to a whisper, but the threat was real. "I will die before I let you marry him."

A knock at the door.

"Rajkumari, the pandit is waiting."

Tara grasped Nayna's trembling hands. "Go."

A single word. A single moment.

And Nayna ran.

ॐ

That night, under the sacred vows and burning flames, **Tara became Queen of a man who would never know the truth.**

As Nayna sailed away into the unkn

own, Tara lowered her veil, hiding the quiet triumph in her eyes.

No man, not even a king, could take away her sister's freedom.

III

The wedding was grand, as befitting a royal alliance. Musicians played their finest melodies, dancers twirled in vibrant clothes, and courtiers showered blessings upon the newlyweds. The people of Nazabgar cheered, believing their beloved princess was riding away towards her new life.

No one knew that beneath the heavy bridal veil, it was not Nayna but Tara.

As the grand procession departed, King Harshat and his veiled bride made their way to his kingdom. The journey was not far, yet the splendor of the occasion demanded an extravagant display. Elephants adorned in gold, horses dressed in silk, and a hundred guards accompanied them.

Tara sat silently in the palanquin, her heart steady, her mind resolute.

The ceremonies in Harshat's palace concluded without suspicion. Tara performed every ritual flawlessly, playing her part as the demure bride. But she knew the illusion wouldn't last forever.

As night fell, a maidservant approached and led her to the grand chambers.

"Pratham Rani, get her ready for tonight," King Harshat's commanded.

The first queen, a regal woman with sharp eyes and a bitter tongue, wasted no time. She removed Tara's veil, her gaze scrutinizing every inch of her face.

"So this is the famed beauty of Nazabgar?" she scoffed, her lips curling with distaste. "The rumors exaggerated. You are fair, but nothing extraordinary."

Tara met her gaze but said nothing. She had expected hostility.

The queen tossed a bundle of clothes into her arms. "Go, bathe. You are to serve the king tonight. Do you understand?"

Tara gave a small nod and took her leave.

ॐ

Alone in the bridal chamber, Tara sat on the vast silk-laden bed, awaiting the moment she knew would come.

The door burst open.

Harshat stormed in, his eyes darkened with rage when he saw the unknown woman.

"Who are you?!" he thundered. "Where is Nayna?!"

Tara rose gracefully, unshaken. "I am Tara, Nayna's elder sister," she said simply. "You demanded King Darshan's daughter, did you not? Well, here I am."

Harshat's fists clenched. "I asked for Nayna!"

Tara tilted her head, her lips curving into an infuriatingly calm smile. "You said, '*Your daughter or war.*' You never specified which daughter."

For a brief moment, Harshat stood speechless, his fury battling his disbelief. Then, with a growl, he turned on his heel, striding towards the door.

Before he could leave, Tara's voice rang out, sharp as a blade.

"Raja Harshat!! . You cannot leave this room tonight."

He whirled back. "And why not?"

She stepped forward, her gaze steady. "Because tonight is our wedding night."

Harshat's expression twisted. "Wedding night? Hah! First night my foot! I will never touch you!"

Tara let out a soft laugh. "Who said I would let you?"

His brows furrowed in confusion. "Then what nonsense are you spouting?!"

She shrugged, walking over to the bed. "Simple. You cannot leave. You will stay here with me."

"Preposterous!" he spat. "If I stay, then what are we supposed to do?! Play chess?!"

Tara stretched her arms lazily before lying down. "Sleep." She grinned. "We will sleep peacefully together."

Harshat's fury knew no bounds. "I will go to the Pratham Rani's chambers!"

He turned again, but before he could reach the door, Tara's voice cut through the air.

"Think again!"

He stopped.

"If you dare to walk out of this room," she smirked, "I will announce to the entire palace that you were unable to... fulfill your marital duties. That you failed to satisfy your new queen and fled in shame."

"No one will believe you" He spat out, but he froze to think about his father.

His body stiffened, eyes blazing. "You dare threaten me?!"

Tara yawned, stretching on her side of the bed. "Oh, stop yelling. You'll wake the whole palace." She patted the empty space beside her. "Now, be a good husband and sleep."

Harshat seethed, his jaw clenched so tightly it could shatter. But Tara knew she had won.

With a furious sigh, he threw himself onto the farthest corner of the bed, turning his back to her.

A slow smile spread across Tara's lips.

The first battle was hers.

౭ఎ

Far away from the grandeur of the palace, a lone figure moved through the darkness.

Nayna—no, **Pihu**—clutched the bundle of supplies tightly against her chest. Hidden beneath the heavy cloak was a letter from Tara, its ink smudged with hurried strokes.

"Remember, Nayna, from now on, you are Pihu. You are no longer the princess of Nazabgar."

Her identity was gone. Her life, erased.

The thick foliage of the mini forest loomed around her, shadows dancing in the moonlight. But thanks to the map Tara had drawn, she managed to find her way. Each step took her further from the only home she had ever known.

By the time she reached the harbor, her legs ached, and her heart pounded with exhaustion.

A worker stopped her at the dock.

"Name?" he asked gruffly.

She hesitated, the name feeling foreign on her tongue. "My name is Nay—" she caught herself. "Pihu. My name is Pihu."

The worker chuckled. "It's the first time I've seen someone struggle to say their own name."

Nayna—no, **Pihu**—forced a small smile and boarded the ship.

She had done it. She had escaped.

But as the night grew darker and the waves rocked the vessel, the weight of her reality crashed down upon her.

She was alone.

Her sister was trapped in a dangerous marriage.

Her kingdom was struggling.

Her people... what would happen to them now?

Fear gnawed at her heart, its claws digging deep.

Curling into herself on the cold ship bunk, she shut her eyes.

For now, she needed rest.

Tomorrow, she would face her new life.

A life where Nayna no longer existed.

IV

The morning sun bathed the outskirts of Great Britain in golden light as Pihu stepped onto its soil. Her breath hitched at the beauty before her—landscapes she had only admired in paintings now went on endlessly before her eyes. A place of dreams, but today, it was the stage for her uncertain reality and future.

She knew the language well, her education ensuring she could have conversations with ease. But her attire, the simple dress of a servant, contrasted against the elegant yet effortless clothing of commoners and the occasional noble passing by. Yet this was not a moment to dwell on appearances—her priority was survival. She needed shelter.

"Excuse me, is there a hotel where I can spend the night?" she asked a female worker, her voice hinted with nervousness.

The woman gave her a kind smile and nodded. "Yes, you can go to the Golden Rose. It's quite popular among travelers." She provided the directions, and Pihu thanked her before setting off.

The Golden Rose was not grand, yet it carried a quiet charm, enough for a temporary shelter. Stepping inside, she approached the receptionist.

"A room, please."

"Here is your key, ma'am. It will be thirty silver coins per night," he informed her.

She nodded, handing over the coins—currency she had already exchanged, though she made a mental note to convert the rest of her wealth soon. Carrying her modest luggage, she stepped into her room.

It was small. Comfortable, yes, but nothing compared to the vast chambers of the palace she once called home. Yet, she reminded herself—she was no longer a princess. Her sister had given up everything for her freedom. She could not let that sacrifice be in vain.

After some rest, she went out, seeking attire that would allow her to blend in. The fine silks and embroidered fabrics she had once worn had no place here. Choosing simple yet elegant dresses, she carefully budgeted her spending. Wealth was not endless, and survival demanded prudence.

As the sun went below the horizon, casting a warm glow upon the town, Pihu returned to her room. Her mind weighed heavy with questions—what skills did she possess that could earn her a living? Politics and sacred scriptures had shaped her knowledge, but they would not put food on her plate here.

Before retiring for the night, she sat by the candlelight and wrote a letter. Though she had no way to send it, the act of writing brought comfort.

❧

"Dear Didi,

How are you, Di? I know you must be adjusting well—you always were like water, flowing effortlessly into any space. I am far from home now, far from Harshat's reach, so you need not worry. But I am afraid, Di. I have found freedom, but will I ever find happiness?

It is late now. Until next time.

Your little sister,

Pihu"

❧

The ink dried as the silence of the night settled in. She secured the letter with her belongings, her heart aching for the warmth of family.

Preparing for bed, she moved toward the door to ensure it was locked. But before she could turn, a sudden movement sent a shiver down her spine.

A man slipped in through the window.

Terror harshed at her throat, her lips parting to scream, but before she could, his rough hand clamped over her mouth.

"Shut up, or I will kill you," he whispered, his voice laced with quiet menace.

Fear froze her in place, and she nodded, her breath shallow. He advanced, closing the space between them until her back met the wooden door.

A knock shattered the silence.

"Excuse me, can you open the door?"

Hope flickered in her chest. Someone was there! But before she could react, the stranger moved swiftly, yanking away her dupatta.

She struggled, muffled sounds escaping her lips. He pulled her into an embrace, his grip tightened, his breath ghosting over her ear.

"Cooperate, and I will leave without harming you," he murmured. "Scream. Sensually."

Confusion clouded her fear. What was he asking of her? When she failed to respond, he reached for the zipper of her kurta, pulling it downward. Panic surged through her veins, and she obeyed instinctively, her cries escaping as broken, desperate moans.

Moments passed. Then, silence.

The footsteps outside faded, and as suddenly as he had come, the man disappeared into the night.

Pihu stood frozen, her chest rising and falling in sharp, uneven breaths.

Who was he? Why had he come?

Shaken, she grabbed her dupatta and pulled it tightly around herself, retreating into the safety of her blanket, dizziness caught up with her. The world outside her palace was far darker than she had imagined. Was this the price of her freedom? Had she escaped monsters only to find herself in the depths of another nightmare?

Tears slipped down her cheeks, and she buried her face in the covers, muffling her sobs.

The night outside stretched endlessly, cold and unforgiving.

Three Months Later...

The scent of fresh roses and jasmine filled the small florist shop where Pihu now worked. A stark contrast to the grandeur of her past life. The once-beloved princess of Nazabgar was now just another face in the bustling neighborhood. A nameless girl selling flowers by the roadside.

Adapting to this new life had been one of the hardest battles she had ever fought. Not just because she had been stripped of her royal identity, but because she had lost the one thing that truly mattered—her family.

She never realized how much warmth her small yet happy home gave her. How the simple presence of her father's wise words, her mother's gentle touch, and her sister's teasing laughter had kept her heart whole. Now, there was no one to talk to at night, no one to hold her when she cried.

Loneliness consumed her like a slow poison.

At first, she had fought through it, convincing herself that she had made the right choice. That this sacrifice was necessary. But as weeks passed, that resolve crumbled.

One evening, as she sat in her tiny rented room staring at the walls that offered no comfort, she asked herself—**for whom am I fighting anymore?**

The answer was silence.

And so, one quiet Sunday morning, she walked to the shore.

The sea roared before her, the waves crashing wildly against the jagged rocks, as if calling out to her. The horizon stretched endlessly, a promise of peace.

Slowly, she stepped forward, allowing the water to wrap around her ankles. Then her knees. Then her waist.

For the first time in a long while, she felt safe.

She closed her eyes.

And let the waves pull her in.

In the grand halls of Harshat's palace, Tara sat comfortably in the royal library, a book resting on her lap. The past three months had been unexpectedly easy. Harshat had ignored her completely, which, to her, was a blessing. She roamed freely, ate what she liked, and did as she pleased without the burden of a demanding husband.

The only thing that plagued her mind was Nayna.

Where are you, Pihu?

She had no way of knowing whether her sister was safe. Their parents, too, remained in blissful ignorance, believing Nayna was hidden somewhere under protection. But Tara knew better.

She needed to find her.

Her thoughts were interrupted by a hesitant cough.

"Ahem."

Tara glanced up, raising an eyebrow. "So, Mr. Akru, what brings you here?"

Harshat stiffened. "Mr... Akru?"

Tara smiled, flipping a page. "You always walk around with such a serious face, I figured you needed a new name to match it."

Harshat's brows furrowed. He had married twenty women, and every single one had longed for his attention. But this one? She barely acknowledged his presence. It frustrated him. This was a marriage he initiated afterall.

"I—I just came to see if you've damaged any of my books," he blurted out.

Tara blinked. "Why in the world would I damage your books?"

He had no answer for that. "N-nothing. I'm leaving." He turned and walked away—too fast, almost as if he was escaping.

Tara shook her head. "Weird man," she muttered, returning to her book. "I don't know what the other queens see in him that they fight for his attention. Anyway..."

She brushed the thought away, but Harshat couldn't.

For the first time in years, someone had dismissed him so effortlessly, and yet, it wasn't that which unsettled him.

There was something about her.

Something familiar.

Something buried deep within the echoes of his past.

That night, Harshat sat alone in his chamber, lost in thought.

His fingers traced the edges of an old wooden box, his most cherished possession. Slowly, he opened it, revealing a faded painting inside.

A painting of a little girl.

His voice was barely a whisper as he spoke.

"Priye... do you know why I feel this way?"

He stared at the portrait, as if it held the answers to his heart's turmoil.

"The only time I've ever felt like this... was when I thought of you."

He sighed, running a hand through his hair.

"I know what love feels like, Priye. And I know I only love you. So why... why do I feel this same pull when she is around?"

The question tormented him. No matter how much he tried to push it away, the feeling lingered like a ghost.

Finally, placing the painting back in its place, he closed the box with a soft thud.

"Good night, Priye," he whispered.

It was a routine he had never abandoned, despite his father's disapproval. And he never would.

At the same time, in her own chamber, Tara lay awake, staring at the ceiling.

Her heart ached with unspoken worries.

"Pihu... are you alright?" she whispered into the darkness.

She could handle everything—this marriage, this palace, this strange life. But the thought of her sister out there, alone and afraid, was unbearable.

Please be safe.

She shut her eyes, holding onto the only hope she had left.

Because a soulmate

wasn't always a lover. Sometimes, it was the bond of two sisters, two halves of the same soul, forever entwined.

The morning sun cast golden hues over the temple courtyard as the newlywed couple stood side by side, fulfilling the sacred ritual. The chants of the priest echoed in the air, the scent of incense mixing with the fragrance of fresh marigolds. Tara bowed her head, accepting the blessings with quiet detachment, her heart elsewhere.

She had done what was required. Now, all she wanted was to return to the palace and disappear into the solace of books and solitude.

As they stepped out of the temple, the waiting carriage stood grandly before them, but something else caught Tara's eye.

A marketplace.

A rush of old memories flooded her—sneaking out of the palace with Nayna, laughing with strangers, bargaining for trinkets. It had been so long since she had felt the simple joy of being among people.

"Is that a market?!" she exclaimed, her voice laced with excitement.

Harshat raised an unimpressed brow. "Yes. Why does that excite you?"

"It has been so long since I talked with people," she grinned, already pulling off her heavy jewelry.

"W-what are you doing?!" Harshat's voice shot up in alarm. His usually composed self faltered at her sudden movements. He turned away, flustered. "Why are you—um—why are you *undressing* before the carriage?!"

Tara let out a loud laugh. "You idiot, I'm not undressing! I'm just getting rid of this weight of jewelleries so I can move freely!"

And before he could stop her, she had already leaped off the carriage and sprinted toward the market.

"Stupid?!" Harshat gawked. "Who are you calling stupid?!"

He had never, in his entire life, seen a queen behave like this. He rushed after her but halted mid-step, turning to his guards.

"Follow her in secret," he ordered. "Do not let anyone near her."

One wrong move, one misplaced step, and she could be in danger.

But when he finally caught up with her, she was standing still, wide-eyed, staring at a small painting stall.

"Why did you run off like that?!" he scolded, his breath slightly uneven. "Do you have any idea how dangerous this is?"

Tara, completely ignoring his words, waved a hand in dismissal. "I know, I know."

Harshat clenched his fists. "Hey! Listen to me when I'm talking!"

"Uff, *Mr. Akru*, let life be fun!" she giggled, and before he could react, she smeared a bit of blue paint onto his cheek.

His entire body stiffened. "You—what did you just—"

"Like this!" she giggled, smearing more paint.

Harshat gaped at her, his anger flickering into something..... foreign. Something that almost felt like... amusement.

"You just wait—!"

He lunged forward, but Tara was already running, laughing as she dashed through the marketplace. For the first time in years, Harshat found himself chasing—not an enemy, not a traitor—but a woman who had somehow managed to pull him into her reckless joy.

He was catching up when she suddenly knocked over a pile of colorful fabrics in his path, making him stumble.

"You little—!" he growled, but his lips twitched against his will.

By now, the guards had discreetly cleared the area, ensuring no threats remained. The empty pathways gave Tara even more room to run, her laughter echoing through the stalls. She spotted a tray of flower petals and, in one swift motion, tossed them toward him.

Petals rained down over Harshat, his usual stern face now covered in streaks of paint and shades of laughter he had long forgotten.

Something deep inside him stirred—**when was the last time I had this much fun?**

But just as he was about to catch her, she suddenly stopped, her eyes locking onto a flower stall.

Hidden behind a wooden pillar, she reached out and gently touched the soft petals.

"Nayna would have loved these," she murmured to herself.

The warmth in Harshat's chest vanished.

The name struck him like a blade, ripping through the momentary joy. **The betrayal. The deception. The sister who stole what was meant to be his.**

His fingers clenched, and without another word, he wiped the paint off his hands and turned away.

"Let's go back."

Tara turned around, confused. "But—"

"No *buts*," he cut her off. His voice was cold again. "We are leaving."

And this time, when he grabbed her hand, there was no trace of laughter left.

☙

That night, Harshat sat in his chamber, the remnants of the day lingering in his mind.

Something about the way she ran, the way she laughed—it haunted him.

He reached for an old wooden box, the one he had treasured for years. With careful hands, he lifted the lid and pulled out a faded painting.

A little girl.

His voice dropped to a whisper.

"Priye... do you know why I feel this way?"

His gaze traced the innocent face on the canvas.

"The only time I ever felt like this... was with you."

His heart ached. Love was not unfamiliar to him. He knew what it felt like. But this—this was something else. A cruel twist of fate.

How could he feel this same pull toward the woman who had deceived him?

Placing the painting back, he exhaled.

"Good night, Priye."

Cold.

Stillness.

Peace.

Pihu felt her body drifting, weightless in the vast embrace of the sea. For the first time in months, the chaos inside her had quieted. The water surrounded her like a lullaby, lulling her into nothingness.

Finally... rest.

But then—

A shadow.

A blur of crimson spreading through the waves.

Red?

Her mind, sluggish and detached, barely registered the color until realization slammed into her like a forceful tide.

Blood.

Her limbs moved before her thoughts did. The survival instinct she had abandoned just moments ago suddenly roared back to life.

She turned, her eyes scanning the water.

A man.

Floating, limp.

His body was marred with wounds, blood seeping into the sea like ink spilling over paper. He was unconscious, his breaths nonexistent.

Before she could think, before she could remind herself that she had given up on life, she was already swimming toward him.

With all the strength she had left, she wrapped his arm around her shoulders and fought against the relentless pull of the ocean.

Her lungs burned, her limbs ached, but s

he didn't stop.

Who was he?

Why was he like this?

The questions could wait.

Right now, all that mattered was getting him to shore.

After an exhausting struggle, Pihu finally managed to drag the unconscious man onto solid ground. The air was crisp with winter's arrival, and the vast shoreline stretched before her. No one was around. Gasping for breath, she let the cold air fill her lungs, grounding herself before turning her attention back to him.

A sharp intake of breath escaped her lips as she noticed the deep wound on his stomach. Blood seeped through his white shirt, staining it almost entirely red. It looked like a bullet wound, but she wasn't sure—guns were rare, something she had only seen a handful of times.

For a moment, she hesitated. He was a stranger, and as a princess, touching a man this way was unthinkable. But this wasn't about etiquette —it was about saving a life. Swallowing her hesitation, she fumbled with the buttons of his shirt, her hands were trembling. When the fabric peeled away, the extent of his injury made her heart race even faster. The wound was deep, and blood was flowing relentlessly.

She needed to act fast. Tearing her dupatta, she pressed it firmly against the wound, layering it with his discarded shirt to slow the bleeding. It wasn't perfect, but it would buy them time. Relief washed over her—he could still be saved.

But just as she moved to get help, a chilling voice shook her relief. "Capture her!"

She turned, heart pounding. A group of masked figures in black surrounded her. Their presence was heavy, their weapons glinting under the pale light. Who were they? What did they want?

Before she could process, three of them lunged forward. Panic surged through her veins, and without a second thought, she ran. The freezing wind cut through her drenched clothes, slicing at her skin like daggers, but she pushed forward. Run. Run for your life.

But they were fast. Too fast.

Within moments, rough hands grabbed her, yanking her back. She thrashed, kicked, screamed—until a sharp strike landed at the base of her neck. Darkness swallowing her whole.

&

A dull ache throbbed in her head when she stirred. Her vision blurred, her body was heavy. Slowly, the world came back into focus.

She was in a small, dimly lit room. The only source of light came from a single high window. Chains rattled as she moved, and a cold realization settled in—her wrists were bound.

Pihu's breath hitched as her gaze fell on the man she had tried to save. He was tied to a chair, his muscular frame rigid even in restraint. But something else sent a shiver down her spine.

Her clothes were different.

Panic clawed at her chest. Who changed her clothes? What had happened while she was unconscious?

A low painful groan drew her attention. The man stirred, his features tensing as he tried to move. His sharp, dark eyes flickered open, scanning the room before locking onto her.

"Who are you?" His voice was deep, rough, yet demanding.

She didn't respond. Her throat felt tight, her mind too clouded with fear and confusion. All she could do was stare at him, her wide eyes brimming with unshed tears.

Before she could find her voice, the door creaked open.

A familiar figure stepped in. The same man who had ordered her capture.

His mask was gone now, revealing a smirking face filled with amusement.

"Well, well," he drawled, crossing his arms. "Both of you are awake."

A low growl rumbled from the man beside her. His entire posture changed, his body tensing with fury. "Steven."

The smirk widened. "Ah, so you do remember me." He stepped closer, his gaze flicking to Pihu. "You were supposed to die," he continued casually, addressing the tied-up man. "But this little bitch saved you." His tone was almost mocking. "So... what is she to you? A lover, perhaps?"

Pihu flinched at his crude words but said nothing. She was listening, absorbing every piece of information she could, desperate to understand the danger she had fallen into.

The man beside her turned his glare toward Steven, his dark eyes burning with barely contained rage. "Let me go. Now. Or you will regret it."

Steven chuckled, shaking his head. "Regret? You must be joking. This is *my* territory. No one can save you. Not your so-called force, not anyone." His laughter filled the room, dripping with arrogance.

But the man smirked. And for the first time, Steven's confidence faltered.

"Laugh while you can," the man said, voice laced with quiet menace. "The people *I* raised is coming for me. And when they do, nothing will save *you*."

As if on cue, a deafening bang echoed from outside. The door burst open, and a frantic figure stumbled in.

"B-boss!" he stammered, face pale with fear. "They're coming!"

For the first time, Steven's smirk disappeared.

VIII

SOne impact sent Steven crashing against the wall, his body shredding under the force of the blow. Before he could recover, an army of armed men stormed the room, their presence suffocating, their guns and weapons gleaming under the dim light.

Pihu barely had time to process what was happening before she saw the man she had saved—now standing tall, his face cold and unreadable.

"I warned you," he said, dusting off his blood-stained clothes as his men untied him. His voice was calm, but there was an undercurrent of steel in it.

A group of medics rushed to his side, tending to his wound with practiced hands. Meanwhile, the others turned their attention to Steven. The brutal sound of fists meeting flesh echoed in the room. Steven barely had the chance to plead before the man gave his final command.

"Don't leave a trace."

Then his gaze fell on Pihu. For a second, she thought she saw something flicker in his dark eyes—something unreadable.

"Take her with us. *Unharmed.*"

And just like that, he turned away, leaving no room for argument.

Pihu didn't fight back. She was too shaken, too terrified, too lost in the chaos of it all. The men surrounded her protectively, guiding her through the dark corridors of the building. The moment they stepped outside, a deafening explosion rocked the earth beneath them.

She gasped, her body trembling as she turned back. The entire building was engulfed in flames, collapsing in on itself like a dying beast.

There was no turning back now.

She had no choice but to follow them.

&

The ride was long. So long that exhaustion began to weigh on her, her body sinking into the seat. The rhythmic hum of the car, the occasional flickering of streetlights outside—it all felt surreal.

Where were they taking her?

By the time they arrived, she was barely awake.

When she stepped out of the car, her breath hitched.

The mansion before her was enormous—nearly as grand as her home in Nazabgar, but where her palace was adorned with royal tradition, this place was sleek, modern, almost intimidating.

A man opened the door for her. "Come with me."

She hesitated but followed.

The double doors swung open, revealing an expansive living room with high ceilings and luxurious furniture. She barely had time to take in the details before one of the men gestured toward a plush sofa.

"Sit. I'll inform the boss."

Pihu lowered herself onto the couch. Her hands gripped the fabric of her dress as she tried to calm her racing heart. Fear was there, yes, but it wasn't just fear for her life. It was something more—something she couldn't quite name.

Minutes later, footsteps echoed from the staircase.

The man she had saved descended, his posture as commanding as before. He didn't sit immediately but studied her with an intensity that made her fidget.

"I heard you saved me." His voice was quieter this time, measured.

She nodded.

"Why?"

The question caught her off guard. She blinked, confused. "Because... you were injured."

His eyes darkened slightly, as if searching for something in her words. Then, without another word, he turned and walked away. But even as he disappeared down the hall, she could feel the weight of his gaze lingering.

Moments later, a butler entered the room, bowing slightly.

"Miss, my master has ordered me to take you to your room."

Pihu stiffened. "What do you mean, my *room*? I'm not staying here."

The butler's expression didn't waver. "I'm afraid it's not up to us."

Frustration bubbled inside her, but arguing seemed pointless. She knew nothing about this place, about these people. For now, she needed to be smart. She needed to find a way to contact her family.

After a moment, she sighed. "Fine."

She followed him through the corridors until they reached a door.

As he pushed it open, she hesitated. "Wait."

The butler turned.

"The man I saved..." she swallowed. "What's his name?"

A small smile appeared on his face. "His name is Andrew."

And with that, he left.

The grand hall was alive with celebration. The annual public giveaway hosted by Raja Hashrat was in full swing, the people gathered in joyous anticipation. It was a tradition—one where both the first queen and the current queen would attend alongside the king.

For Tara, it was the first time she saw the grand queen without the weight of sorrow upon her. The last time they met, she had been grieving, a ghost of herself. But today, she stood tall, regal—blooming like an elegant rose.

Everything was perfect.

Until it wasn't.

A sudden movement from the crowd. A flash of steel.

Tara's heart lurched.

A man lunged toward the king, a knife gleaming in his hand. The knights reacted, but they were too slow. The blade was already descending, aimed straight at the king's back.

Gasps filled the air, people screamed, chaos erupted—but in that split second, before the blade could strike—

Tara moved.

She didn't think. She didn't hesitate.

She threw herself forward, the knife sinking into her stomach instead.

Pain. Blinding, burning pain.

Her body stiffened, her breath hitched. She barely registered the panicked cries around her, barely felt herself stumble.

"Tara!!"

A strong pair of arms caught her before she hit the ground.

The king's face was pale with shock, his grip on her tightening as he lowered her carefully. His eyes darted to the blood spreading across her dress, his own breath unsteady.

The attacker had been captured, but he didn't care.

He only saw *her*.

"You..." His voice was hoarse. "You always said you hated me. So why? *Why* did you take the blow for me?"

Tara's lips trembled. Her vision blurred, but she forced herself to speak.

"Because..." She inhaled sharply, her body trembling against the pain. "Because the people here... they see you as their king. If they saw you fall... they would be afraid."

And then, the darkness took her.

Her body went limp in his arms.

"Tara? *Tara*!!"

He shook her gently, his hand cupping her cold cheek. Her head lolled slightly, her breathing shallow.

"Hey—keep your eyes open! *Stay with me!*" His voice cracked, desperation creeping in.

The world around them blurred. The event was immediately shut down, the people ushered away, but the king paid no attention.

He lifted her into his arms, his grip secure, his expression set with grim determination.

"Get the physicians *now*!" He barked, his voice echoing through the palace as he carried her inside.

He wouldn't let her die.

He *couldn't*.

IX

The palace was in chaos as they rushed Tara back to her chambers. Servants scurried through the halls, whispering prayers, their eyes filled with worry.

Harshat stayed beside her the entire time, his pace uncharacteristically urgent. His breath was uneven, his grip tight. The weight of her limp body in his arms felt heavier than it should.

Why?

Why did it matter so much?

The moment they reached her chambers, he gently laid her down on the silk-covered bed. "Call the doctor! *Now!*" His voice, usually commanding, carried a rare note of panic.

He stood by the bedside, watching as the physician examined her wound. His hands curled into fists.

"The wound is not life-threatening," the doctor finally said, his tone reassuring, "but it is still severe, Maharaj."

Harshat exhaled slowly, his tense shoulders lowering slightly. Relief, foreign and unfamiliar, settled in his chest.

The doctor turned to his assistant, retrieving a small vial from a satchel. "Maharaj, I will need your assistance. The medicine must be applied at a precise angle."

Harshat nodded and moved without hesitation. He slipped an arm under Tara's back, lifting her gently against him. Her head lolled onto his shoulder, her warmth pressing against his skin.

"Everyone, leave," he ordered. The room emptied in an instant.

The doctor hesitated for a moment before continuing his work. "You will have to hold her steady, Maharaj."

Harshat glanced at the unconscious woman in his arms. A flicker of hesitation crossed his face as he whispered, "I apologize for touching you without your permission."

His hands moved with practiced ease, unbuttoning the fabric carefully. He was no stranger to battle wounds, but something about this moment felt different.

As the doctor applied the medicine, Tara stirred, a deep frown forming on her sleeping face. Then—

A sharp sting.

Her body reacted instinctively, her nails digging into his back. The pain barely registered to him, but the intensity of it made his breath hitch. Her grip was desperate, as if seeking an anchor through the agony.

The physician worked swiftly, binding the wound with clean bandages.

"She must rest for a few weeks before resuming any duties," he advised before bowing and stepping out.

Harshat glanced down at her. The pain had eased from her features, replaced by peaceful slumber.

For a moment, he simply watched her—watched the way her chest rose and fell in steady rhythm, watched the way her lips were slightly parted, as if lost in a dream.

A dangerous thought crossed his mind.

Would she have done the same for him... if she didn't care at all?

Shaking his head, he called for the maids. Keeping her limp body on the bed.

"Take care of her," he instructed. Without another word, he turned and walked away.

୫୦

When Tara woke, the pain in her stomach was dull, manageable. Her body still ached, but the sleep had worked wonders.

She stretched slightly, wincing, but pushed through.

The first thing she did was summon a servant. She needed to know what happened "What happened after I collapsed?"

The young girl hesitated, then answered, "The king carried you to your chambers. He... he was very worried about you, Rani-sa."

Tara frowned slightly. Harshat? *Worried*? That didn't seem right.

She dismissed the thought—until the next words left the servant's lips.

"You scratched his back badly, Rani-sa. It was bleeding."

Tara stiffened.

She had hurt him? But he still helped her?

A strange sensation stirred in her chest. Guilt? Perhaps. But more than that—something else. Something she couldn't quite define. Trust? Maybe.

"I don't like owing people," she murmured, pushing the covers aside.

She wasn't the type to sit idle.

൭

She needed to find him.

She asked around the servants, who in return gave some same answers.

"We don't know Rani sa"

"You should rest Rani sa"

"The emperor would be mad at us if he gets to know you got out of bed"

Finally, she found him in his chambers, standing near the window, a large painting in his hands. The late afternoon sun cast golden light over his sharp features, making him look almost lost in thought.

She cleared her throat. "*Ahem.*"

Harshat turned, his dark eyes meeting hers.

"What do you want?" His voice lacked its usual edge.

Tara stepped further inside, arms crossed. "Is this how you treat the person who saved your life?" she teased, a small smirk playing at her lips.

Harshat scoffed. "No one told you to play the hero."

She raised a brow, unimpressed. "Regardless, I did."

She approached, her gaze flickering toward his posture—stiff, tense. His hand hovered near his back, almost as if he was subtly trying to ease the pain.

She sighed. "Sit."

Harshat narrowed his eyes. "Why?"

"I heard I scratched your back. Let me put medicine on it."

He let out a dry chuckle. "I can do that myself."

She crossed her arms. "I don't need anyone's favor! Just *sit* down."

He stared at her for a moment, something weird flashing across his face. Then, without another word, he sat on the bed, turning his back to her.

Tara took the small jar of medicine from the nearby table and dipped her fingers into it. The cool ointment met his skin, and he inhaled sharply.

She worked carefully, massaging the wounds gently.

His back was broad, marked with scars that told stories of battles fought long before this one. But among them, four fresh red lines stood out. Some of them still bled.

She swallowed.

Her fingers unconsciously softened their touch.

Harshat didn't say a word.

The silence stretched between them, thick with something unspoken.

Then—her eyes flickered to the painting he had been holding earlier.

Something about it felt... familiar.

Harshat noticed her movement and, before he could react, she reached for it.

The moment she saw it, her breath caught in her throat.

Her hands trembled as she traced the edges of the frame, her eyes widening.

"This..." Her voice came out barely above a whisper.

Harshat stiffened.

Her fingers tightened around the painting.

"What is my lost childhood painting doing here in *your* room?"

X

Days passed, each one blending into the next. The same dull routine—eat, roam, sleep. Pihu felt like a caged bird, her wings clipped before she even had a chance to fly. She missed her family, her sister.

Every time she asked about Andrew, the answers were the same—silence or a dismissive shake of the head. The servants, the guards, even the butler refused to tell her anything.

And when she tried to step beyond the mansion's towering walls, the guards blocked her path without a word.

Frustration burned inside her.

What did he want?

Why was she here?

And why wouldn't he *face* her?

The questions gnawed at her until she couldn't take it anymore.

So, she planned. She observed. She waited.

And finally, two weeks later, she found her escape.

At the far end of the rose garden, hidden behind thick vines and overgrown bushes, there was a broken section of the wall. Crumbling bricks, just wide enough for her to slip through.

She planned for days on how to divert the attention of gaurds, and then slip into that, she did it.

Heart pounding, she climbed over. The thorns scratched her skin, but she didn't stop.

The world outside was vast—open roads stretching endlessly before her. The cold wind bit at her skin, but she didn't care. She was *out.*

She ran.

And ran.

Until exhaustion weighed her down, until her feet ached and her breath came in ragged gasps.

But freedom was short-lived.

Before long, she was caught.

Strong arms grabbed her, holding her in place. No matter how much she struggled, it was useless. The inevitable loomed over her like a dark cloud.

But this time, when they dragged her back, **Andrew was there.**

He sat in his chair, the dim light casting shadows over his sharp features. His gaze was unreadable, detached—like she was nothing more than an inconvenience.

"So?" His voice was calm, almost bored. "What do you want to say to me?"

Pihu clenched her fists, her entire body trembling—not just from the cold but from anger, frustration, *helplessness.*

"Why are you keeping me here?" she demanded, her voice breaking slightly. "Why won't you let me go?"

Andrew exhaled slowly, tilting his head. His gaze flickered over her—mud-streaked skin, bare feet red from the cold, strands of hair sticking to her damp face.

"You're shivering," he noted flatly. "We'll talk inside." , he turned and walked away.

She had no choice but to follow.

❧

Inside, the warmth of the mansion was suffocating after the bitter cold outside. She sat stiffly on the couch, her body tense as Andrew settled across from her.

"So?" She gritted her teeth, her voice firmer now. "Now tell me."

He leaned back, utterly at ease. "You can ask whatever you want about me," he said, his tone as casual as if they were discussing the weather. "Except to release you."

Her jaw tightened. Fighting him was useless, she knew that now. She needed answers first.

"What's your full name?"

He smirked. "Andrew."

She frowned. "Full name."

His smirk deepened. "My first name is enough to make people scream, princess."

Her heart skipped a beat. *Did he know?*

Did he know she was a runaway princess?

She swallowed hard but nodded, refusing to let fear show. "Who *are* you?"

He gestured lazily for one of his men to bring a blanket, then turned back to her.

"Mafia."

The word hung in the air, heavy, unshakable.

A shiver ran down her spine.

"Am I in danger?" she asked, her voice quieter now.

Andrew considered her for a moment before answering.

"Yes. If you consider me one." His eyes shifted slightly. "If not... then no."

Pihu exhaled shakily. There was no real comfort in his words.

She hesitated, then said, "Can you help me with something?"

Andrew raised an eyebrow, then chuckled under his breath.

"Someone," he called out lazily, "help her with whatever she wants."

Then, just like that, he stood up.

Pihu blinked in disbelief. "Aren't you going to listen to my request?"

He straightened his coat, adjusting the cuffs, then walked towards her.

Before she could react, he placed his hands on her shoulders and guided her to back down onto the couch. His touch was firm, unyielding, yet strangely careful.

Then he leaned in.

His hands pressed against the couch on either side of her, trapping her in place. Their faces were close—too close.

His voice dropped to a whisper.

"Relax, princess."

Pihu's breath hitched.

"My men will handle whatever you need," he continued, his gaze unwavering. "I have work to do."

And then—his lips curled slightly.

"But you?" His voice was softer now, almost dangerous. "You're staying with me until That disappears."

His eyes gleamed with something unreadable.

"Maybe even after that."

Pihu froze, her heart hammering against her ribs.

Andrew straightened, giving her one last lingering glance before turning away.

"Let's go," he ordered his men.

And just like that—he was gone, leaving her in a flustered, confused mess.

Tara's fingers trembled slightly as she clutched the old painting. The faded colors, the delicate strokes—it was undeniably *hers*.

Her childhood. A memory she thought was long lost.

Her heart pounded as she turned to Harshat, searching his face for answers. "What is my lost childhood painting doing here?!"

Harshat's gaze sharpened at her outburst. "What do you mean *your* painting?" he asked, standing up.

"This one," she insisted, holding it up. "Why do you have this?"

He was silent for a moment, then answered, his voice wavering, "A girl gifted it to me when I was a child."

Tara frowned. That didn't make sense. Why would anyone give *this* specific painting to *him*?

"I see…" she murmured, her eyes tracing the familiar brushstrokes.

A thick silence settled between them. The weight of unspoken words pressed against her chest.

Harshat's voice broke the stillness. "Why do you ask?"

Her grip on the painting tightened. She hesitated. How could she even begin to explain?

"Its…" she stuttered, then inhaled sharply.

"Its what?" he pressed, stepping closer.

Her throat felt dry. "It's… *me*," she finally admitted.

"In the drawing." A lie, but she needs to know how intentions first.

Harshat's expression shifted—his stoic mask cracking for just a second. But then, just as quickly, it was gone.

Tara held her breath, waiting for his response.

But none came.

☙

Pihu folded the letter carefully, sealing it before handing it to the butler. "Make sure my sister gets this," she pleaded.

The butler bowed respectfully. "Of course, Miss."

A weight lifted from her chest. At least Tara would know she was alive.

For the first time,

Days turned into weeks, and something unexpected happened—she and Andrew started to *talk*.

Not as captor and captive.

But as something else, friend.

He would sit with her in the evenings, watching her try new foods she had only read about in books. He would laugh—*actually laugh*—when she scrunched her nose at the strange flavors.

He treated her like a queen. Gentle, indulgent... attentive.

Until she mentioned leaving.

Then, the warmth in his eyes would vanish, replaced by something cold, and distant.

But no matter how well he treated her, Pihu *had* to leave.

Because this place—this country—wasn't her home.

Her home was in **Nazabgar**.

Where her mother and father waited. Where her sister, *Tara*, still lived. Where she belonged.

She missed them. She missed their voices, their laughter.

Yet, no matter how many times she tried to bring it up, Andrew would only watch her, silent.

His sharp eyes would lock onto hers, studying her, searching for something she couldn't understand.

And then, without warning, he would bring his face dangerously close to hers.

So close she could feel his breath against her skin.

So close her heart would stutter in confusion.

And then... he would release her.

As if testing something.

As if waiting for something.

Pihu found it *strange*.

But she needed him.

If she ever wanted to see her family again, she needed his help.

&

Andrew leaned against the window, swirling the amber liquid in his glass, his expression stoic.

He had lost count of how many people he had killed.

Blood on his hands was nothing new.

Becoming the boss had been simple—one clean shot. The man before him had been powerful, yes. But not to *him*.

Still, something had been bothering him lately. A single question.

One that refused to leave his mind.

It had happened during his last job.

The target had been an aristocrat, an official who had done no real wrong. But in Andrew's world, innocence didn't matter.

Money did.

He had been quick. Precise.

A bullet to the lungs. A fatal shot, but slow enough for the man to feel it.

As the official lay on the ground, choking on his own blood, he had looked up at Andrew with an amused, almost pitying smile.

"You've never saved anyone, have you?" the man had rasped.

Andrew frowned. The words had caught him off guard.

The official coughed, blood staining his lips. IIis body trembled as life drained out of him.

"Killing people is easy," he whispered, his voice barely above a breath. "But if you had real guts... if you were truly *brave*..."

He gasped, struggling to inhale.

"...you'd try saving someone."

Andrew had watched, silent.

The man's smile turned weak. His eyes, glazed with death, flickered with the last spark of defiance.

"If you can't..." His voice was barely a whisper now.

"You're still weak."

A choked laugh.

"***Loser***."

And then, that—he was gone.

Andrew had stood there, staring at the lifeless body.

He had heard a lot of last words. Most people begged, cursed, or simply screamed.

But this?

This was different.

And for some reason, it *stuck.*

The thought gnawed at him, creeping into the cracks of his mind.

Had he ever saved someone?

Did it even matter?

His grip tightened around the glass as his gaze flickered toward the locked door.

Toward **her**.

Pihu.

He had planned to kill those lifeless brown eyes.

But not yet.

Not until he brought them back to life.

Not until he saw the light return to them.

Because only then—only when they were truly *alive*—would he destroy them.

And that?

That would be *fun.*

XII

Harshat's brows furrowed as he tried to make sense of her words.

"What do you mean it's *you* in the picture?" His voice was laced with confusion. Was she insane, or was there really a chance that she was *the girl*—the one he had been searching for all these years?

Tara's grip on the painting tightened. "That's what I asked *you.* Why do you have this in the first place? Even if someone gave it to you long ago, why are you still holding on to it?"

She didn't know what unsettled her more—the fact that this painting, *her painting*, had somehow ended up in *his* possession, or the possibility that he had been *treasuring* it all these years.

Was he some kind of obsessive creep? She wouldn't be surprised. Looking at the sheer number of wives he had taken, anything was possible.

Harshat scoffed, still trying to process everything. He tried to take the painting back "Why do you care?" His voice had an edge to it, but he subconsciously reached out for the drawing.

His mind raced. Could it really be her?

For years, he had searched for the girl who gave him this painting. A piece of his past that refused to fade. And now, *she* was standing before him, claiming it as hers?

Before Tara could press him further, he swiftly took the painting from her hands.

"You should rest," he said, his tone returning to its usual arrogance. "Or else people will think I'm such a loser that I used my *twenty-first* wife as a shield and overworked her until her stitches reopened."

Tara narrowed her eyes, whispering. "People wouldn't be wrong about that."

"What?!"

"Nothing," she giggled to herself, turning away. "I'll go for now because I **am** tired. But we *will* talk about this painting. A *real* conversation. You *do* know how a conversation works, right?"

Harshat's lips pressed into a thin line. "Of course, I know. We talk."

She chuckled, shaking her head. "Yeah, *we both* talk. Not just *you*. Goodbye."

Without waiting for a response, she walked away, leaving Harshat staring at the painting in his hands.

&

A soft knock echoed in Tara's chambers.

"Rani Tara? May I come in?"

Tara quickly hid the half-written letter beneath a pile of papers. It was meant for her parents—an attempt to explain the tangled fate that had separated their daughters.

"Come in," she answered.

The door creaked open, revealing a poised woman dressed in elegant silk. Tara recognized her as one of the king's many wives, though she had never spoken to her in person before.

"I imagine you're still unfamiliar with the customs of this palace," the woman said, her voice calm and composed. "It has been three months, but I was occupied with responsibilities, so I had to delay this."

Tara gave a polite nod, offering a small smile. She had noticed how busy the palace had been, though she still didn't fully understand *why*.

The woman gracefully sat down across from her. "I am **Kashi**, the *Pratham Rani*—the first queen."

Tara straightened at the revelation. *So, this is the King's first wife...*

"There are nineteen other *ranis* in the palace," Kashi continued, "and you will meet them soon in the *Puja Ghar*." She gestured to a young girl beside her. "This is **Shanti**. She will be your guide until you learn your way around."

Tara's eyes flickered toward the girl, who bowed respectfully.

Kashi's gaze softened. "Every week, we gather to pay respects to the King's father. Due to your injuries, we have postponed your *Pehli Rasoi*."

There was kindness in her tone, but Tara couldn't shake the sadness hidden in her eyes.

"The *Pehli Rasoi*?" Tara hesitated, unsure if she should ask questions. One wrong word could land her in trouble.

"It is a tradition," Kashi explained. "A new queen prepares her first meal for the royal family and court as a symbol of her acceptance into the palace."

Tara nodded slowly. Another unfamiliar tradition she had unknowingly walked into.

"Get ready," Kashi instructed. "Shanti will escort you to the *Puja Ghar*." Then, she turned to the girl. "Make it quick."

Shanti nodded, bowing once again.

Getting dressed was an ordeal with the bandages restricting her movements.

As Shanti helped her, the weight of everything that had happened in the past few months finally crashed over Tara like a tidal wave.

Her **home** was gone.

Her **freedom** was gone.

Her **family**—Pihu, her parents—were far, far away.

And now... she was a queen in a palace she knew nothing about, bound to a man she barely understood.

The realization hit her all at once.

"No!"

The sudden outburst startled Shanti, who flinched. "Nai Rani Sa? Did I hurt you while changing the bandages?"

Tara barely heard her. She was too busy staring at her reflection—her face, perfectly made up, hiding the evidence of sleepless nights and silent cries.

Her voice dropped into a whisper. "No, it's just..."

Her breath hitched.

"...the Maharaj saw and *touched* my naked back." almost whispered.

Her face burned in mortification.

Shanti let out a small chuckle. "He is your husband. It's only natural."

Tara turned away, gripping the edges of the dressing table.

"That's true... but..."

She couldn't finish her sentence.

Shanti only smiled. "Come, *Nai Rani Sa.* It's time."

ॐ

The *Puja Ghar* was filled with the low hum of prayers and the scent of burning incense.

Due to her injuries, Tara was instructed to wait outside the *Garbhagriha*, the sacred sanctum where no bloodshed or injury was allowed.

She sat on a cushioned seat, watching as the *ranis* gathered inside.

Her gaze wandered until it landed on a golden crib placed nearby.

Inside, a tiny baby girl, barely five months old, kicked her legs in the air, playing with her own fingers.

Tara felt an unexpected warmth spread through her chest.

A baby.

Was she... *his* child?

Perhaps the daughter of **Pratham Rani?**

She leaned closer, brushing her fingers against the infant's tiny hand. The baby cooed, grasping her finger in a soft, delicate grip.

Tara's lips curved into a gentle smile.

"She is beautiful," she murmured to one of the attendants. "Is she *Pratham Rani's* child?"

A voice behind her answered before the attendant could.

"No."

The firmness in the tone made Tara turn.

It was **Kashi**.

Tara's brows knit together. "No?" She glanced back at the child. If not **hers**, then whose?

Kashi's expression rem

ained stern, but something in her voice held a quiet sorrow.

"She is *our* sautan."

Tara's breath caught.

Not a child.

A **wife**....?

XIII

Tara's breath hitched. She stared at Kashi, searching her face for some sign that this was a cruel joke.

"What... do you mean?" Her voice wavered, her heart pounding against her ribs.

Kashi's expression remained eerily calm, as if she had repeated this truth too many times to still feel its horror.

"I mean exactly what I said," she replied. "She is our *sautan*—our co-wife. The **tenth** Rani of this palace. The wife of Maharaj Harshat."

Tara's gaze snapped back to the golden crib. The tiny girl lay there, innocent and unaware, her tiny hands grasping at the air.

"But... she's just **five months old**." Her voice barely escaped as a whisper, her stomach twisting in revulsion.

Kashi stepped forward, brushing a gentle hand over the baby's soft hair.

"I told you I would introduce you to all the *ranis*," she said. "Since you've seen **Rani Bela** first, let me explain."

Tara could hardly process the words.

"She was given to the **king's father** as part of a treaty from Pratappur. The rulers of that state feared an invasion, so they offered a marriage in exchange for peace. The king's father agreed." Kashi's voice remained steady, as if she had long buried her horror beneath layers of obedience.

Tara's hands clenched into fists. *A treaty?*

"A marriage **to an infant?**"

Kashi nodded solemnly. "Originally, it was meant to be the eldest Rajkumari, **Lata**. But she died suddenly. So instead... they sent **Bela**."

Tara felt like the world had tilted on its axis.

An infant. Married off like cattle.

Her hands trembled as she took a step back, bile rising in her throat.

"What about..." Her voice faltered. She didn't want to ask—**she didn't want to know.** But she had to. "Their... their *wedding night?*"

She saw the answer in Kashi's eyes before she even spoke.

"It was done."

Tara's breath left her body.

"The **king's father** was present to ensure it."

Her vision blurred, the walls closing in around her.

Disgust. Rage. Nausea.

The emotions warred within her, suffocating her like thick smoke. She wanted to **scream**. She wanted to **run**.

How could anyone—**how could he—**

"This is hell," she whispered, more to herself than anyone else.

Kashi exhaled slowly, the years of silent suffering visible in her every movement.

"You'll get used to it," she said. But there was no conviction in her words. Only resignation.

༄

Kashi led Tara toward the gathering of other *ranis.*

Tara's heart clenched as she took them in—

Five of them in their **late teens.**

Eight of them barely in their **early teens.**

And the last **five... were children.**

Children.

Girls no older than **eight or ten**, standing in delicate silks, their faces holding an innocence that had no place in this cursed palace.

Tara felt the world tilt again.

This wasn't marriage.

This was **madness**.

Her stomach twisted as she thought of **Harshat**. She had known he had multiple wives, but this? **This?**

What kind of man was he?

Her mind reeled back to that *painting*—her sister's face in *his* room.

What kind of twisted **pleasure** did he find in it?

The thought alone made her skin crawl.

She wanted to **laugh**. To **cry**. To **vomit**.

But all she could do was stand there, trapped in this waking nightmare.

☙

A commanding voice cut through the air.

"Everything is done with the **puja**, yes?"

An older woman stepped forward, her presence demanding immediate obedience.

"Yes, Teacher," Kashi answered.

Tara's gaze settled on the woman—**the teacher of the ranis.**

Her face bore only the earliest signs of aging, wrinkles just beginning to form, suggesting she was somewhere in her forties.

She studied Tara with an unnerving intensity, her thin lips curling into a smile that sent a chill down Tara's spine.

"So," she murmured, stepping closer, "you are the new queen."

Tara could do nothing but nod.

Something about the woman's gaze made her uneasy. A knowing smirk played on her lips, as if she had seen this cycle repeat too many times.

The teacher turned away, addressing the attendants.

"Prepare her."

Tara stiffened. "For what?" she said on cue

The teacher didn't answer. Instead, she continued, **"Her and Rani Amba. They will both serve the King in his bath today."**

Tara's breath stopped.

"Serve?"

Her stomach dropped.

What did that mean?

Her pulse thundered in her ears, but no one around her seemed surprised. The other *ranis* barely reacted. As if this was **normal**.

Tara wanted to

run.

But there was nowhere to go.

The walls of this palace had already begun closing in.

Hell, no, maybe worse than that.

XIV

Tara and Rani Amba were prepared in silence.

The **eighth** Rani was only **thirteen**.

She sat beside Tara, wrapped in layers of a deep green saree—the king's favorite color, as the teacher had explained. Their hair was neatly tied up, adorned with fragrant flowers. The scent of jasmine and sandalwood filled the air, but to Tara, it smelled of something far worse—**submission**.

She had been given **orders**.

Due to her injuries, she was not to step into the tub. Her only task was to mix flowers and essence oils into the water **once the Raja arrived**.

She had no idea what Amba's role was.

Then the doors creaked open.

Raja **Harshat** entered, stepping into the massive marble tub. But something was strange. His **eyes were covered** with a satin blindfold.

Tara's stomach twisted.

What kind of sick game is this man playing?

But she **stayed silent**.

She was new here, and she needed to **lay low**. *Observe. Learn.*

She dipped her fingers into the cool water, carefully pouring in the fragrant oils and rose petals. The room was eerily quiet. The king's presence felt heavy, like a coiled snake ready to strike.

Then, she **looked up**.

Her body **froze**.

Across from her, **Amba stood bare, the green saree pooling at her feet.**

Her frail body trembled, yet she moved forward, her steps hesitant but practiced.

Tara's breath **caught in her throat.**

Her heart **pounded.**

For a moment, she felt like she was outside her own body, watching this nightmare unfold **from adistance**.

Then— **rage.**

White-hot, **blinding rage.**

Before she could even think, she **moved**.

She lunged forward, **grabbing Amba's wrist and yanking her away.**

"Get up. Come on!"

The sudden movement sent a sharp pain through her injured back, but she barely noticed.

Amba stumbled, eyes wide in terror.

Tears streamed down her cheeks. **She didn't fight back**. She didn't even flinch.

Tara's grip tightened.

She snatched the saree from the floor and *wrapped it around the girl's trembling frame.*

"Are you okay, Amba?"

The girl opened her mouth, but *no words came out.*

Her lips quivered. Her restless, tear-filled eyes **spoke volumes.**

Tara pulled her into a tight embrace, pressing the girl's head against her shoulder.

It will be alright.

That's what she wanted to say.

But would it?

Hearing the horror was one thing. **Watching it unfold** was another.

A **roar** shattered the silence.

"What is happening here?!"

The teacher's furious voice rang through the bathhouse.

Tara turned, her pulse steady despite the storm inside her.

Harshat had removed his blindfold, standing **motionless**.

His expression was unreadable.

The teacher's eyes blazed with **fury**. "How dare you interrupt the king's bath?!"

Tara ignored her, **locked eyes with Harshat,** and spoke with authority.

"Ekaant."

The word echoed through the room.

The servants hesitated.

"I want to speak to the King. **Alone.**"

One by one, they obeyed.

All except *her*.

The teacher **did not move.**

Tara turned her gaze to the woman, her voice sharp as a blade.

"I thought you were learned enough to know that when a **royal member** demands *ekaant*, all others must leave."

The teacher's jaw tightened. "I am the **Queen's Teacher**. You cannot—"

Tara cut her off, stepping forward.

"And I am the Queen. You are a paid servant. **Leave.**"

The woman's face twisted with fury.

"But—"

"Out. Now."

For a moment, the air stood *still*.

Then, with a reluctant bow, the teacher turned on her heel and left.

Now, it was just the three of them.

Tara. Amba. Harshat.

Silence filled the room, save for Amba's soft, muffled sobs.

The girl clung to Tara's arm, **her tiny body shaking**.

Harshat said nothing. **Just stared.** into nothingness.

Tara moved.

Her feet carried her forward, toward the *mighty king*.

And without a second thought, she **slapped** him across the face.

The sharp **crack** echoed through the chamber.

Harshat's head snapped to the side.

He didn't move.

For a moment, *even the air held its breath.*

Then— *he spited.*

"How dare you strike a **King**?" He didn't shout, he just.....stated.

Amba **flinched**.

Tara?

She **stood firm.**

"King?" she scoffed, voice dripping with disgust.

"Just sitting on a throne doesn't make you a king."

She took a step closer.

"Marrying twenty-one wives doesn't make you a king."

Another step.

"Disgracing children to fulfill your sick pleasures doesn't make you a king."

Harshat's fists clenched. *His body shook with rage.* because only he knew the truth.

Tara did not care.

"Only a coward—a *namard*—does these things while pretending to be a ruler."

His lips parted, his anger barely restrained. He wanted to speak, but can't.

But Tara was done listening.

She turned to Amba, took the girl's hand in hers, and walked away.

"I'm taking her with me," she declared, voice unwavering.

"This is a matter of the *andar mahal*. You have no right to interfere."

And without another glance, she led Amba out of the bathhouse—leaving the *so-called King* behind.

The soft rustle of fabric filled the air as the servants gently wrapped Amba in fresh, dry clothes. Tara sat nearby, wincing slightly as another set of hands carefully tended to the wound on her back. The sting barely registered. She was still replaying the scene in the bathhouse, still feeling the weight of Amba's fragile body trembling in her arms.

"You should not have helped me, the elders are going to scold you" Amba spoke with caution.

"You should return to your chamber now, get some rest," a voice suggested. Tara.

Amba hesitated before nodding. "Yes, I'll return... Please take care of yourself too."

Their eyes met, an unspoken promise exchanged. Tara watched as Amba disappeared into the dimly lit corridor, her small figure swallowed by the flickering shadows.

A moment later, a servant approached, bowing deeply.

"Rani Tara, the **Father King** requests your presence for tea."

The words were polite, but their meaning was clear. *A serious conversation.* A summons.

Tara inhaled sharply.

"I'm on my way," she said.

Could she refuse? No. Refusing was never an option.

ॐ

The path to his chamber was long.

The Father King had grown too weak to move freely, so he held court in his bedroom—a **sanctuary ofpower** despite his frail body.

Tara's thoughts swirled like a raging storm.

I did the right thing.

But would others understand?

Would **he** understand?

She had defied Harshat without fear, but this was different. The Father King was **not a man to be challenged lightly.**

The moment she arrived, a servant pulled back the heavy curtains.

"Please enter, Rani Tara. The Father King is waiting."

Tara swallowed her nerves and stepped inside.

The room reeked of **authority**.

Even in disarray—messy blankets, unruly hair, the scent of fading incense—the Father King radiated power. Gold dripped from the walls, the afternoon sunlight casting long shadows across the floor.

Tara bowed deeply.

"Pranam, Rajpita."

His sharp, assessing gaze pierced through her.

"Arise."

His voice was gravel, weathered but commanding.

"So, you are the twenty-first Rani?"

Tara nodded, eyes lowered.

He exhaled, fingers tightening around his teacup.

"Three months in this palace and already causing a ruckus!"

The cup slammed onto the floor, shattering.

Tara did not flinch.

"How dare you interfere?! Do you have any idea how much effort I put into handling that girl? And now *you*—you are adding to my burdens!"

Fury rolled off him in waves.

Tara's nails dug into her palms. Her hands were *sweaty, shaking.* But she held her ground.

You did the right thing.

The Father King took a deep breath, exhaling through his nose.

"But..."

His gaze darkened.

"I'll forgive you. **Once.**"

A beat of silence.

"You saved him from that attack."

Then, a dismissive wave of his hand.

"Now, get out of my sight."

Tara bowed—because she had to.

Because defiance had limits.

As she turned to leave, she caught a flicker of movement from the corner of her eye.

A shadow soldier stepped forward.

"Any instructions, My King?"

A pause.

The Father King leaned back against the pillows.

"No. Let's see... what her *existence* does to this palace."

The soldier nodded and disappeared into the shadows.

Tara walked away, her heart hammering in her chest.

ॐ

The days passed in uneasy silence.

Tara rested. Healed. The wound on her back faded, but the tension in the palace did not.

Harshat had requested an audience with her many times.

She refused.

Not until she was ready.

Now, *she was.*

There were too many unanswered questions.

The painting. The Father King's cryptic words.

And the **man behind it all.**

All thoughts surrounding her brain as she sat in front of the mirror

As she finished getting ready, Pratham Rani Kashi entered.

"You look gorgeous," Kashi murmured.

Tara turned, surprised by the sudden visit.

"Thank you," she replied with a soft smile.

Kashi's gaze drifted downward, **fixating on the necklace around Tara's neck.**

A stunning piece—gold, with **green** gemstones embedded into the intricate design.

Kashi's fingers hovered over the necklace, her expression changed to solemn.

Then, her voice trembled.

"Don't wear this."

Tara blinked.

The shift in Kashi's tone was subtle, but *it wasn't a request.* It was a plea.

"But I like it—"

"It *doesn't* suit you. Your dress is blue." Her gaze lingered on her neck.

Kashi unclasped her own necklace—a delicate **blue** sapphire piece—and placed it in Tara's hands.

"Take this. It will match your dress better."

Tara hesitated.

How could she take something that belonged to **her**?

The **First Queen. The Maharani.**

"I—"

"Take it," Kashi interrupted.

Her lips curved into something between a smile and a wound.

"Sharing... has become a habit."

And then, she walked away.

Something was weird, but she couldn't quite define it.

Harshat was already seated when Tara arrived.

The tension between them sat thick in the air.

"Sit," he ordered.

She did.

"So," he started, leaning back. "What do you want to talk about?"

Tara took a slow breath.

So many questions burned inside her.

But she needed to be careful.

"Did you meet father?" A flicker of surprise crossed her face.

"I did."

Harshat's brows furrowed. "What did he say?"

Tara held his gaze.

"Nothing important. Just scolded me for interfering."

Silence stretched between them.

Where should she start? The most important thing,

Then—

"You remember the painting, right?"

Harshat tensed.

"Yeah. You wanted to talk about it."

She leaned forward.

"Will you answer honestly if I ask?"

He scoffed.

"I'll answer what I want. Whether you believe it or not... not my problem."

Tara narrowed her eyes.

"Fine. Tell me—how did you get that painting?"

Harshat exhaled, fingers tapping against the table.

"When I was ten, my father took me on a hunting trip near Mrigpara. We disguised ourselves, camping near the jungle. One night, I slipped away. Found myself in the village fair."

His voice lowered.

"I had never seen one before. I wanted to explore."

He paused, as if debating whether to continue.

"I caused a... commotion. To escape, I ducked into a small tent. Inside, I met a girl."

Tara's pulse quickened.

"And?"

"She gave me the painting."

His words *sharpened, clipped.*

Like he didn't want to say more.

Tara frowned.

Who was this girl?

And *why* did she have a portrait of her, Nayna?

"But why do you still have it?"

Harshat's fist slammed onto the table.

"Never. I would **never** throw it away."

His chest heaved.

"Because she's—"

He stopped.

Tara leaned in.

"She's...?"

Harshat clenched his jaw.

"She's someone I need to meet again."

His voice dropped to a whisper.

"To say something."

Then, as if realizing he had revealed too much, he snapped—

"Now , **leave**."

Tara stood, lips curling in amusement.

"You know," she mused, tilting her head.

"When you were younger, they should have called you '*Akru Kumar*' instead of *Rajkumar*."

His eyes burned.

Tara stared.

And walked away.

Kashi watched from the shadows.

As Harshat stormed past her, she called out—

"Akru Kumar?"

Her voice

soft, *longing.*

He brushed past her.
"I'm not in the mood, Kashi."
She watched him walk away.
Her heart clenched.
"Why don't you look at me the way you look at her... even when I wore green? Even when I did what she did?you hated seeing blue, but you told her nothing"
"Why... why...?"

XVI

The teacher took a week off to let her anger subside. In her absence, the palace was filled with an unusual sense of relief. The young ranis, who once dreaded her rigid and unsettling lessons, now laughed freely, their days unburdened by the suffocating presence of their instructor.

Tara sat cross-legged on her bed, engrossed in the words of her book. Yet, an unsettling sensation crawled up her spine—someone was watching her. She whipped her head toward the door, but the dimly lit corridor beyond was empty. Shaking her head, she forced herself to dismiss the feeling. "I'm just being paranoid," she murmured. Perhaps the tension in the palace was getting to her.

But the sensation returned, prickling her skin like the lingering touch of unseen eyes. This time, she stood up and shut the door firmly, pressing her palm against the cold wood as if sealing away her unease. Though no one could see her now, the feeling refused to dissipate. Her book, once a welcome distraction, now felt heavy in her lap, unreadable.

Sighing, she pushed it aside and decided to take a stroll in the garden.

The garden stretched before her, bathed in the soft glow of the evening sun. Vibrant flowers swayed with the breeze, their fragrance mingling with the damp earth beneath her feet. This place had always been a comfort—an oasis of serenity amidst the palace's rigid walls. It reminded her of Nazabgar, of carefree days spent playing with Nayan, her closest friend.

But today, even here, the sense of being followed clung to her like a shadow. She took a deliberate step forward. The crunch of gravel beneath her feet was immediately echoed. She stopped. The echo stopped.

Tara's heart quickened.

Hidden figures peeked from behind pillars and foliage, their movements betraying their presence. As she resumed her walk, the faint jingling of her payals reached their ears, signaling her movement. The unseen followers stiffened, whispering amongst themselves.

Then, in an instant, Tara vanished.

"Where did she go?" one of them whispered, craning her neck. The group of young ranis searched frantically, their wide eyes scanning the garden.

"I'm here."

A collective gasp rippled through them as Tara dropped down from the tree above, landing effortlessly before them. The girls stumbled back, startled.

"Why were you following me?" she asked, amusement twinkling in her eyes.

One of them, still catching her breath, blurted, "Aap rani hain ya bandar?!"

Tara giggled, twirling the delicate flower in her fingers before playfully tapping it against the girl's nose. "Bandaron ki rani hoon," she declared, trying to crack a joke. "Now tell me, what's going on?"

The ranis exchanged uneasy glances. Just as one of them opened her mouth to speak, their expressions suddenly shifted—eyes wide with alarm. Without another word, they turned on their heels and fled.

Tara frowned, watching them disappear into the corridors. "Weird..." she muttered.

She turned—and collided with something solid.

A firm chest.

Before she could hit the ground, strong arms caught her, steadying her mid-fall. Tara blinked up, her breath hitching.

Harshat.

"Now what drama are you planning?" His voice was laced with irritation. "Try to live peacefully in the palace, will you?"

Tara scowled, pulling herself upright. "Oh my god, are you a thief or what, Akru Kumar?! Why do you walk so silently? Do you enjoy sneaking up on people?"

Harshat's jaw clenched. "You're impossible! First, you call me Akru, and now a thief?!"

She folded her arms, standing her ground. "Anything wrong with that? Look, the girls ran away because of you." Her frustration deepened. It had been the first time the young ranis had approached her willingly, and now, thanks to this insufferable man, they had fled.

Without another word, she turned on her heel and strode back toward her chambers.

Harshat exhaled sharply, shaking his head before stalking off in the opposite direction—only to bump into Kashi.

"Oh god!" he groaned, rubbing his forehead. "That girl's face is unlucky—I keep running into people today!"

He stomped off, muttering curses under his breath. Kashi simply watched him go, her expression a mix of amusement and something sad.

❧

The chamber was dimly lit, the flickering oil lamps casting elongated shadows on the stone walls. The young ranis huddled together, their voices hushed.

"What should we do?" one of them whispered.

"I don't want to go back to those awful lessons," another shuddered. "They scare me."

"But what choice do we have? The teacher holds too much power. Only Rani Tara dared to speak against her, but I..." she hesitated, voice faltering, "I don't have that kind of courage."

A heavy silence followed.

"Should we ask Tara?" someone suggested hesitantly.

"Ask me what?"

A startled gasp rippled through the group as they turned to find Tara standing behind them, arms crossed, an eyebrow raised.

They exchanged nervous glances before Amba finally stepped forward. "Tara... we don't want to attend those classes anymore. Can you help us?"

Tara's expression softened. "Of course, I will. I don't want them either."

But how? That was the real question. The teacher was no ordinary woman. She had been a formidable presence in the palace long before the current grand queen had even come of age. With years of experience in governance and finance, she wielded an influence that surpassed most of the queens themselves.

"We need a solid plan," Tara mused.

They all sat in a circle, brainstorming ideas. Suggestions were made and discarded, frustration mounting with each failed attempt. Then, suddenly, Tara turned to one of the girls.

"Rani Vaishali, you're the princess of Talahpur, right?"

Vaishali nodded, surprised. "Yes... why?"

"Do you know the ancestral teachings of your kingdom?"

Vaishali's brows furrowed. "Yes, of course..."

Tara's lips curled into a knowing smile. "Good. Listen carefully."

The room fell silent as Tara unfolded her plan. As the details unraveled, the young ranis exchanged glances—hesitant at first, but soon, nods of agreement spread through the group.

By the time Tara finished speaking, determination gleamed in their eyes.

"Now," she commanded, standing up, "return to your chambers quietly. Begin the preparations."

As the girls dispersed, Tara watched them with a smirk.

"Ab kuch aise hoga," she murmured

to herself, "jisse Pratham Rani khud unhe bahar fenk nikalengi."

A storm was coming. And Tara was ready.

XVII

The afternoon sun slanted through the tall windows, casting golden streaks across the polished floors as Tara approached the grand queen's chamber. She knocked gently.

"Rani Kashi?"

A soft rustling of fabric, then the door opened. Kashi's face, serene yet distant, greeted her with a small smile. "Oh, Tara. Please, come in."

The scent of fresh parchment and ink filled the air, evidence of the queen's earlier work. She set her papers aside, guiding Tara to a set of plush sofas near the open balcony. A warm breeze carried the scent of jasmine and something sweeter—something rich and comforting.

Kashi inhaled, pausing mid-step. "Oh my, what is this sweet smell?"

Tara's lips curled into a small smile as she placed a silver bowl on the table between them. "Kheer. I made it for you."

Kashi blinked in surprise. "For me?"

"You gave me such a precious necklace," Tara continued, nudging the bowl toward her. "I thought I should offer something in return. You don't lack anything, so this is all I could think of—something homemade, something from me. Please, have it."

The sincerity in Tara's voice unsettled Kashi. She looked down at the bowl, the creamy kheer glistening under the light. She should have felt pleased, touched even. Instead, guilt curled inside her like a serpent.

Tara's gratitude was genuine, but Kashi knew the truth—the necklace had not been given out of kindness. It had been a move, a desperate attempt to soothe her own jealousy, to suppress the ache that clawed at her heart every time she was reminded of her husband's indifference. How much longer would she endure this? How much more pain would she have to swallow before she won even a sliver of his love?

She forced a small smile. "That was thoughtful of you, Tara. But it wasn't necessary. And even if you wanted to give me something, you could have just sent it through a servant."

"That wouldn't have been the same," Tara countered softly. "I wanted to see your reaction."

Kashi hesitated, then reached for the spoon. Just as she dipped it into the kheer, the door burst open.

"Maharani-sa!!"

A breathless servant stumbled in, wide-eyed with panic. "Please, come quickly! Rani Rudraveena—she collapsed! She won't wake up!"

The spoon clattered against the bowl as both queens shot to their feet.

"Where is she?" Kashi demanded.

"This way!"

Tara and Kashi followed at once, their hurried steps echoing through the corridors.

৪৩

Rani Rudraveena lay motionless on the bed, her fragile body wracked with tremors. Her once radiant skin had taken on a sickly bluish-green hue, her breathing shallow, her lips barely parting as she shivered beneath the silk sheets.

A cluster of queens and palace women stood around her, their hushed murmurs laced with fear. The teacher, an ever-imposing figure, remained at the foot of the bed, her expression unreadable.

Kashi's voice cut through the tension. "Where is the Raj Vaidya?! Call the palace doctor immediately!"

Servants scattered at her command.

"What happened?" she turned to the teacher, demanding an answer.

The teacher's usual air of confidence flickered, just for a moment. "She came to me, seeking advice about the previous lessons," she said slowly. "We spoke briefly... and then she collapsed."

Her sharp gaze swept over the room, her fingers tightening around the edge of her dupatta. Something felt off. Years spent navigating the politics of the palace had trained her instincts well—there was something unnatural about this, something beyond a mere fainting spell.

"Pratham Rani!"

The urgent call came from Rani Vaishali, who had been examining Rudraveena closely. She rose, her face pale yet determined.

"This is **poison**."

A collective gasp rippled through the room.

Kashi's heart pounded. "Poison?"

Vaishali nodded grimly. "As you know, Pratham Rani, I am the princess of Talahpur—our kingdom is renowned for its knowledge of plants and their effects. At first, I sensed something was wrong from afar, but now, having examined her, I am certain. She has been poisoned with a rare plant, one that acts as an aphrodisiac but is deadly for young girls. If given to all of us, only you and Rani Tara would survive."

Silence fell over the chamber, thick and suffocating.

This was no accident.

For the first time in the history of the palace, an attack had been made on the queens.

৪৩

The doctor arrived swiftly, administering medicines to stabilize Rudraveena's condition. Slowly, the chaos began to subside. One by one, the queens dispersed, murmuring their prayers before leaving.

Only Kashi, Tara, Vaishali, and Rani Amba remained behind, lingering in the dimly lit room. The silence between them was heavy, each lost in troubled thoughts.

Then, suddenly—

A soft retching sound.

All eyes snapped to Rani Amba as she clutched her stomach, her face contorted in pain. Before anyone could react, she lurched forward, vomiting onto the floor.

The sharp scent of bile filled the air. Servants rushed to clean up, while the doctor hurried to her side, offering her medicine.

Kashi's hands trembled at her sides. First Rudraveena, now Amba.

What in the gods' name was happening?

She clenched her jaw. Was this an attack? If so, who was behind it? What was their motive?

Her thoughts spiraled until Amba, still weak, spoke in a hoarse whisper.

"Pratham Rani..."

Kashi's gaze snapped to her. "Yes?"

"I think I know who did this."

Tara stepped forward, helping Amba sit up properly. "Tell us."

Amba swallowed hard, her face pale. "It's the teacher," she rasped. "She made those laddoos. After everyone left, I took a small bite in secret. A few minutes later... my whole body felt numb. You saw the rest."

The room tensed.

Kashi's breath came short. The teacher?

The woman who had been in the palace before even the grand queen herself? The one entrusted with governance, with the very foundation of the palace's teachings?

"Ranisa," Tara's voice was firm. "I saw her making those laddoos too. When I visited the rasoi , she was preparing them. Call it a request or a demand—but I want her out. After today, I do not feel safe around her."

Kashi's mind warred with itself.

It was impossible. And yet, the weight of two suffering queens, of the growing unease in the palace, of the frightened gazes of the younger girls—it all pressed against her, demanding an answer.

She looked around the room, at Tara, at Vaishali, at Amba's pale face.

Then, slowly, she exhaled.

The decision had been made.

The teacher had to go.

XVIII

Her reaction was swift, almost desperate. "Lies! Your Highness, I never gave her those laddoos! She brought them herself!"

Tara's eyes narrowed. "Are you calling Rani Rudraveena a liar? Why would she put poison in her own food?"

The teacher's face darkened with frustration. "You! Ever since you arrived, strange things have been happening!" Her voice trembled, not with fear, but with the anger of someone who knows their power is slipping. "You must have done something!"

Kashi's hand slammed against the wooden armrest of her seat. "Are you in your senses, Teacher? First, you claim that Rani Rudraveena poisoned herself, and now you accuse Rani Tara?" Her sharp gaze bore into the older woman. "She was with me before the incident. She made kheer for me with her own hands. We were together in my chambers when all of this unfolded."

The teacher turned on her heel, pointing an accusatory finger at Tara. "And you don't find that suspicious? She made food for you too, My Queen! She could have poisoned you as well!"

A flicker of something dark passed through Kashi's expression before she stood. "Enough," she said coldly. "I saw her taste the kheer before serving it. If there was poison, she would have been affected first."

"Exactly," Rudraveena added, her voice quieter but just as cutting. "She is innocent. You, on the other hand, have been named in this crime. And I know what I felt. That poison was not in my hands when I walked into your room. But when I left..." Her voice trailed off, the implication clear.

A verdict was forming. The shift in power was palpable, like a tide rising against the once-feared teacher.

Kashi took a deep breath, her decision final. "You have been accused of poisoning a queen. Whether intentional or not, the fact remains that she was nearly killed under your care. Given the lack of evidence for a harsher punishment, I strip you of your position as palace teacher for life."

The teacher gasped, as if the words themselves had struck her.

"You have one week to leave the palace," Kashi continued, her voice unyielding. "You are no longer welcome here."

A wave of relief rippled through the room. It was done. The reign of the cruel teacher had ended.

✸

Days earlier, in the dim glow of lantern light, Tara had gathered her allies.

"Rani Vaishali," she had asked in hushed tones, "can you prepare a poison that looks deadly but has an antidote?"

Vaishali had nodded without hesitation. "Yes. I know of herbs that will turn the skin blue and weaken the body, but the antidote will cure it within seconds."

Tara's lips curled into a satisfied smile. "Perfect."

She turned to Rudraveena. "I need you to take the poison."

The young queen's breath hitched. "Me?"

Tara's gaze was steady. "It has to be you. If I do it, they'll suspect something. You are the eldest among us. Your word carries weight."

Rudraveena swallowed hard. "I... I'm scared."

Tara took her hands. "I know. But this is our only chance. If we do this right, we will never have to suffer through those wretched lessons again."

Rudraveena took a shaky breath, then nodded. "Alright."

And so the plan unfolded.

The poisoned laddoos were placed in the teacher's room. Rudraveena ate them there, ensuring suspicion would fall in the right place. Vaishali watched over her, waiting for the moment to administer the antidote.

Amba played her part flawlessly, feigning illness to further tarnish the teacher's image. And when the moment came, Tara seized it, turning the court of queens against their oppressor.

Justice had been served, even if the truth was buried beneath layers of carefully spun deception.

❧

The news spread through the palace like wildfire. The woman who had ruled the lessons for so many years—who had wielded influence like a sword—was gone.

Some celebrated her downfall. Others whispered in hushed corners, their voices tinged with fear and disbelief. But no one dared challenge the grand queen's ruling.

Not even the king.

The palace functioned on unspoken laws. Just as queens had no say in the courtroom, the men had no authority within the inner palace. Kashi's word was final.

Tara walked the corridors, a quiet satisfaction blooming in her chest. The plan had worked. The girls were safe.

As she stepped into her chambers, a servant rushed in behind her. "Nai Ranisa, a letter has arrived from Videsh."

Tara's heart leaped. *Could it be…?*

"From outside India?" she repeated, excitement bubbling in her voice. "Bring it to my study table at once!"

She turned to leave, already imagining the familiar handwriting, the words waiting to be unfolded—when a voice stopped her in her tracks.

"Tara."

She turned, her breath catching as she met the piercing gaze of Harshat.

He stepped closer, the weight of unspoken words lingering between them. His expression was unreadable, but his voice was quiet, sincere.

"Thank you."

It was just two words. Simple. But something about them made her heart stumble.

She blinked, momentarily lost for a response. But before she could say anything, Harshat turned and walked away, leaving her standing there—wondering why those words felt heavier than any victory she had won that day.

Tara stood frozen for a moment, watching Harshat's face with a mix of suspicion and intrigue. His voice, steady but urgent, held something different tonight—something almost raw.

"*Thank you?*" she echoed, tilting her head slightly. "Thank you for what?"

Harshat stepped closer, close enough that she could see the faint shadow of worry under his eyes. "I've thought through some things because of you," he admitted, his voice softer now, less guarded. "Can we talk?"

There was a vulnerability in his gaze that caught her off guard—gone was the smugness, the arrogance that usually draped his words. Instead, his eyes, dark and searching, looked almost... desperate. *Like a boy trying to prove he isn't as bad as they say.*

Tara hesitated. "We can, but—"

Before she could complete her sentence, he cut her off, his tone almost pleading. "Please. Don't say no." His hands clenched at his sides, as if forcing himself to keep from reaching out. "After so many years, I finally feel something real—this feeling of being judged fairly, of being understood. Just hear me out. Once. Please."

Tara's sharp gaze lingered on him, searching, dissecting, trying to find a trace of deception, an angle he could be playing. But she found none.

"Fine," she relented, voice measured. "But not now. Meet me at the balcony garden tonight."

Harshat exhaled, almost as if he had been holding his breath. He gave a quick nod and turned away, vanishing down the corridor.

But he left something behind. A ripple in Tara's thoughts, a nagging curiosity she wasn't sure she wanted to entertain. *What had he realized?*

Just yesterday, his anger had been simmering beneath his words. He had interrupted her conversations with the other queens, shadowed her movements, throwing barriers in her path. *And now, this?*

She shook her head, pushing it aside. There was something more important now.

The letter.

Her heart skipped a beat as she turned on her heel and hurried to her study table. The wax seal was still intact, the paper smooth under her fingers. The moment she cracked it open, a delicate, familiar scent filled the air—rosemary.

Pihu.

Her hands trembled slightly as she unfolded the letter, her eyes devouring the words written in elegant strokes.

Dear Didi,

It's been so long since we've seen each other. How are you? Have you been able to adjust in that wretched palace? How are Mom and Dad? I'm sure they worry about us every day. But what can we do? Fate has played such a cruel joke on our once-happy lives.

Don't worry about me, Di. The first few days were difficult, but a kind man let me work in his household. They provide lodging for their staff, so I have a place to stay. I'm surviving. But I worry about you.

Are you okay?

He said that after two months, I can take a short leave and visit home. If that happens, we will meet, okay? And if I can help it, I won't return to England. But... do I even have that choice?

There is so much more I want to say, but the page is running out of space. So much to share, yet so little room.

Write back to the same address. If it reaches me once, perhaps we can talk more often. I miss home so much.

I love you.

Pihu.

৪১

The letter ended, but Tara's emotions did not. A tight knot that had been sitting in her chest for months unraveled. Her vision blurred as the first tears fell, then another, until she was clutching the letter against her chest, her body trembling with relief.

She was alive. She was safe. *Pihu was safe.*

All those sleepless nights, the horrible scenarios that had plagued her mind, the fear that her little sister had been lost to an unforgiving world—gone.

But alongside that relief, another worry crept in.

Harshat.

Even though the marriage had bound them, even though she had secured a place in this grand palace, Harshat was still Harshat. A known womanizer. If Pihu returned now, who was to say he wouldn't set his sights on her? *Would he make her his 22nd queen?*

No. She wouldn't allow that.

She wiped her tears quickly, pushing away the thought, and grabbed a blank sheet of paper. She needed to reply.

৪১

Dear Pihu,

I just received your letter. You don't know how relieved I am to hear that you are safe.

Your knowledge of English is truly useful now—I knew all those hours you spent learning would come in handy someday.

I don't know how long it takes for these letters to reach you, but I will let you know when it's safe for you to return. Letters are secure; once sealed, no one reads them.

I will write to Mother and Father as well. They will be overjoyed to hear from you.

Stay safe. I will write again soon.

Tara.

☙

She quickly folded the letter and began another, one for their parents, ensuring them of Pihu's safety.

Once done, she called for a trusted servant.

"Mahi, deliver these to the postman. No one else is to see them. Understood?"

The servant nodded, but Tara wasn't one to take chances. She leaned in slightly, her voice dropping to a warning whisper.

"Remember, I have eyes on your family."

Mahi's face paled. Of course, it was a bluff. But Mahi didn't need to know that.

☙

A Balcony of Petals and Shadows

The palace was quiet by the time Tara made her way to the balcony garden. A soft, cool breeze kissed her skin, carrying the faint scent of roses and sandalwood.

But it was the sight before her that made her steps falter.

The table was set—ornate yet intimate. A blend of Indian and Western elegance. Candles flickered on its surface, their golden glow casting long, dancing shadows against the stone walls. And scattered across the floor, woven into the setting—rose petals.

She hadn't expected this.

A frown tugged at her lips. *Was this some kind of game?*

She stepped forward cautiously and sat at the chair, the silk of her saree rustling in the quiet. The night stretched on, stars twinkling above her, the palace a silhouette against the moonlight.

She waited.

And waited.

Until—

A shadow moved at the entrance.

She turned, her pulse quickening.

There he was.

Harshat stepped into the light, his face unreadable, his presence heavy.

For the first time, Tara wasn't sure if she was facing the man she despised... or someone entirely different.

XX

"Sorry I'm late..."

Harshat came speed-walking into the candlelit balcony, the soft glow casting long shadows across his face. He pulled out the chair across from Tara, sinking into it with a weary sigh. Strands of his dark hair clung to his damp forehead, the heat of the day still lingering on his skin.

"I'm the one who called you here, but the court work delayed me," he admitted, rubbing the back of his neck. His voice carried exhaustion, but there was something else beneath it—urgency.

Tara studied him for a moment. His normally composed demeanor was slightly shaken, but she wasn't sure why. She straightened in her seat. "It's alright. Court matters should be your priority anyway." She folded her hands in her lap, then met his eyes. "Why did you call me here?"

Harshat sat up, shoulders squared. "To be honest with you. Completely. I want you to know the truth—everything I know, everything I feel."

His voice had changed. Gone was the charm, the easy arrogance she had grown used to. This was different—serious, raw. Tara's legs crossed instinctively, a habit she had when bracing herself for something intense. Her fingers curled tightly together in her lap.

"Go ahead," she said, her voice steady.

Harshat inhaled deeply, as if summoning the strength to peel away years of silence.

"Here goes nothing..." he murmured under his breath before beginning.

"Tara, first of all, I want to thank you—and the others—for kicking that teacher out. I hated the way she forced those lessons, the way she tried to turn everything into seduction. It was suffocating."

Tara's brow furrowed. That wasn't what she had expected. She knew about the teacher—the older woman who had been tasked with 'educating' the queens in ways that disgusted them all—but why had Harshat tolerated it if he had hated it so much?

"You're the king," she said, tilting her head slightly. "If you despised it, why allow it? Who could possibly force something like that on you?"

Harshat's jaw tensed. He held her gaze for a long moment before finally speaking again.

"Let me start from the beginning."

Tara listened, the weight of his words pressing against her chest, unraveling the image of Harshat she had always held in her mind.

"I was in love once," he confessed, a sad, almost bitter smile touching his lips. "When I was young, I met a girl. I promised myself that if I ever married, it would be her and only her. But fate..." He shook his head. "Fate had other plans."

Tara said nothing. She only nodded, encouraging him to continue.

"When I turned fourteen, my father decided it was time for me to marry. He brought in portraits of princesses, dozens of them, and told me to choose my bride." His fingers tightened into fists on the table. "I refused. I only wanted the girl in the painting I had seen. When I still hadn't agreed after a year, he forced me to marry Rani Kashi."

Tara's breath hitched slightly.

"I was fifteen. She was thirteen."

A cold shiver ran down her spine.

"We didn't know what marriage was. We were just children. But we became friends—best friends, partners in crime. We were happy in our own way. Not as husband and wife, but as two people who had each other's backs." His voice softened for a moment. "That was enough for me. Until it wasn't."

Tara felt a growing tension in the air as he continued.

"When I turned eighteen, my father demanded that Kashi and I produce an heir. But... I couldn't." He exhaled sharply, shaking his head as if the memory still haunted him. "I cared for Kashi, but not as a man should for his wife. She was my friend, my family. I couldn't bring myself to touch her like that."

He fell silent for a moment, his fingers threading through his hair in frustration.

"When I refused, my father was furious. He saw it as disobedience, a failure of duty. And so, he forced me into marriage again. Then again. And again." His voice grew bitter. "With each new wedding, the brides became younger. He believed the younger the girl, the more obedient she would be. But they were just children, Tara. Children."

A wave of nausea twisted in Tara's stomach.

"I was powerless," Harshat admitted. "Even when I became king, I held no true authority. My father kept his power through the shadows, controlling everything. I had nothing." He leaned forward slightly, his eyes pleading, desperate for her to understand.

"He made sure I would give him an heir, no matter the cost. He sat by my bedside, Tara. *He watched*." Harshat's voice broke slightly, his hands pressing into his temples. "The night I was meant to consummate my marriage with Bela, he placed a chair beside my bed. The white curtains were drawn, but I could feel his presence. He stayed there all night to ensure I 'performed my duty.'"

A sickening feeling coiled in Tara's gut.

"I couldn't do it. I **wouldn't** do it." His voice turned hollow. "I faked it. I pinched Bela to make it seem real. She was so scared... but at least she was safe that night."

Tara's breath came in shallow bursts. The room felt smaller, suffocating.

"That's when he brought in the teacher. To teach the girls how to *please* me, how to *seduce* me." Harshat let out a broken laugh, shaking his head. "I wanted power so I could stop this. But even when I became king, I realized—I still have none."

He reached out then, taking her hands in his. His grip was firm, but trembling.

"Tara, I love you. I want to be with you. I *want* to make you happy." His voice cracked slightly. "I know this palace is filled with horrors, but please... give me a chance. Help me end this. Help me give the girls a better life. Please."

Tara's heart pounded against her ribs. She wanted to pull away. She wanted to scream, to tell him that it was too late, that she would never love him, that none of this changed anything.

But it *did* change things.

The image she had held of Harshat for so long—the heartless king who collected women like ornaments—was crumbling before her eyes.

Tara pulled her hands free, rising abruptly from her seat. The air felt thick, her mind spinning in endless loops.

"I don't know if I can give you a place in my life," she whispered. "But I do know those children deserve better."

And with that, she turned and walked away.

She didn't stop until she was deep within the palace, her breaths uneven, her thoughts colliding.

The painting. The girl he loved was Nayna. He thought it was me.

The weight of it all crushed against her chest.

Then—

A sound.

A quiet, muffled sob.

Tara turned her head, following the soft sniffs. She stopped at a half-open door, her fingers hesitating before pushing it open.

Inside, sitting on the edge of the bed, her body trembling with suppressed cries—

Rani Kashi.

Her tear-streaked face lifted, eyes bloodshot, pain radiating from every inch of her.

Tara stepped inside, her voice softer this time.

"Pratham Rani Kashi... what happened?"

A bitter laugh escaped Kashi's lips as she wiped at her swoll en eyes. "Pratham Rani, huh?" She reached for Tara's hand, squeezing it slightly.

"Let's talk," she said.

Kashi's fingers gripped Tara's shoulders tightly, her nails pressing just enough to convey the raw desperation coursing through her veins. Her body trembled with barely contained emotion, her breath hitching between quiet sobs. Without a word, she guided Tara in front of the grand mirror that stood tall against the wall, its surface reflecting more than just their outward forms—it held years of unspoken grief, shattered dreams, and unfulfilled love.

"Look at the mirror," Kashi's voice was hoarse, her throat worn from crying. "Tell me, who do you see?"

Tara blinked, momentarily confused by the question, but answered nonetheless. "Me. Tara."

The grand queen nodded slowly, her lips curving into a fragile smile—one that held no warmth, no joy.

"Tara," she repeated softly. "Raja Harshat's 21st wife."

Then, with deliberate slowness, she stepped aside and stood before the mirror herself. The shift in reflection felt heavier than it should have, like the weight of her entire existence had just taken center stage. Her bloodshot eyes met Tara's through the mirror, the desperation within them piercing, suffocating.

"And now?" she whispered, her voice laced with unspoken agony. "Who do you see?"

Tara hesitated. "...You, Rani Kashi—"

"Yes," Kashi let out a bitter chuckle, her smile twisting into something painful. "Pratham Rani Kashi."

She let the words hang in the air, hollow yet deafening. Then, stepping forward, she turned to Tara, her gaze searching, demanding an answer that would never come.

"You are the 21ˢᵗ queen," she said, her voice trembling yet firm. "You have not even been married for six months, yet you—*she*—received the one thing I yearned for all these years."

Tara swallowed, her mind reeling.

Kashi's fists clenched, her nails biting into her palms, but she barely seemed to feel it. "Tell me, Tara," she pleaded, her voice cracking under the weight of her sorrow. "What do I lack? What do you have that I don't?"

She took a shaky breath, her chest rising and falling with emotions she could no longer control.

"I did everything they wanted me to do," she continued, her voice rising with each word, as if years of restraint were finally crumbling. "I took responsibility for the inner palace, cared for the other queens, shared my husband without a single complaint. And yet—**"why are you the one receiving the love I have craved for so long?"**

Tara's breath hitched, a cold chill creeping up her spine.

"Every other queen knew," Kashi went on, her eyes glistening, "that they had to divide their love. But I? I was meant to be his *one and only*. I dreamed of a life with my husband, my *love*, mine and mine alone." She swallowed thickly. "I thought... I thought that if Raja Ji and I held hands, we could face anything together. But instead, I—"

Her voice wavered dangerously, then finally broke.

"Pehli rani hokar bhi, dusri aurat bane rahe hum."

Tara closed her eyes. *"Even though I am the first queen, I have been the second woman my entire life."* Ringed in her ears.

Silence filled the room, heavy and suffocating.

Kashi stood still, her breath uneven, her body trembling as if she could no longer bear the weight of her own existence. Then, in a voice so quiet it was nearly swallowed by the vast emptiness of the chamber, she asked—

"Why?"

Tara had no answer.

Her mind was spinning, drowning in the impossibility of it all. Harshat loved the girl in the painting—**Nayna**. But he thought that girl was *her*. Kashi had loved Harshat from the beginning, had devoted her life to him, yet he had never looked at her the way she had wanted him to. And Harshat—he wanted the girls to have a safe life. He wanted *her* to help him fix the mess of a kingdom that had trapped them all.

Where did that leave her?

What was right? What was wrong?

She hated being the cause of anyone's suffering. It went against everything she had ever believed in. *Dhruv Tara*—the North Star—shining brightly at birth, meant to navigate those who were lost. She was meant to *guide*, not to be the reason someone felt adrift.

But if she chose Kashi...

She saw Amba's face again—terrified, desperate, broken. The image of that young girl, trembling in fear, haunted her every time she tried to lean towards one decision.

Tara could no longer breathe in that room. Without another word, she turned and walked away, leaving Kashi with nothing but her shattered heart and unfulfilled love.

๛

A Night of Reflection, A Morning of Decision.

Tara locked herself in her chambers that night.

She extinguished every candle, shut every curtain, drowning herself in darkness. She dismissed the guards, sent away the servants, allowing no disturbances. Alone, she sat, her thoughts spiraling like a storm that refused to settle.

If I accept Harshat, I betray Kashi.

If I choose Kashi, I condemn the young girls to a life of horror.

There was no easy answer. No painless choice.

Her heart ached, but she knew one thing for certain—her emotions would not cloud her judgment. A decision made in haste, in weakness, was never a wise one. She had chosen to marry Harshat in a moment of clarity. And she would choose her path now with the same precision.

Tara did not sleep that night.

By dawn, her mind was clear.

The sun rose, golden light spilling into the halls of the palace. And with its rise, a decision was made.

Tara dressed carefully, her posture unshaken, her walk steady. The uncertainty of yesterday had been replaced with quiet determination. The guards who had seen her shaken and lost the night before now watched her stride past them with an air of confidence they had never witnessed before.

She had a plan.

And she was going to execute it.

When she reached the doors of the royal chamber, the guards bowed. One of them stepped forward. "Shall I announce your presence to the Father King?"

She tilted her head slightly, offering a knowing smile. "No need."

The guard entered the chamber, speaking in hushed tones. A moment later, the heavy wooden doors opened.

Inside, the room was just as it had been the last time—grand, intimidating, suffocating. But this time, she wasn't afraid.

The Father King sat upon his throne-like chair, his presence looming, his aura one of unquestionable authority. His sharp, calculating eyes flicked toward her as she stepped forward.

"Pranam, Rajpita," she greeted, bowing her head with practiced grace.

He observed her, then motioned for her to raise her head. "Tell me, what is it that you wish to discuss, 21st Queen Tara?"

Tara smiled. Not the gentle, polite kind. Not the nervous kind.

A smile filled with intent.

Without waiting for permission, she strode forward and seated herself on a chair near him, crossing one leg over the other.

A silent challenge.

For the first time, the Father King's eyes narrowed ever so slightly.

Tara rested her hands in her lap, tilting her head slightly.

"Let's make a deal, old man."

XXII

The Father King lounged on his gilded chair, fingers tapping impatiently against the carved wooden arms. His belly—plump from years of indulgence—tightened slightly as he let out a sharp, irritated breath. His small, calculating eyes flicked toward Tara, his lips curling in disdain.

Then, with a sudden burst of fury, he slapped the armrest.

"How dare you!" he bellowed, his voice booming through the chamber like a crack of thunder. "You rude, insolent girl! Do you have any idea the trouble you'll be in if I call the guards?!"

Tara remained utterly unfazed. She met his rage with an easy, almost amused expression, as if she had expected this reaction.

"Yes, Father King," she said smoothly, folding her hands in her lap. "I know exactly how much power you hold in this palace." A pause. A slow, deliberate smile. "But call me when you hear the news. I'll be ready to make a deal."

The old king's brows furrowed. His fingers, which had been clenched in a fist, relaxed slightly. *News? What news?*

His beady eyes narrowed in suspicion. "What do you mean by that? What deal?" he demanded.

Tara stood, brushing imaginary dust from her dress as she prepared to leave. She glanced back at him, her voice calm but firm.

"Let's have a meeting after two weeks. You'll understand everything by then."

With that, she turned on her heel and walked away, leaving the Father King in silent confusion. He could have called the guards, could have pressed her for answers—but he didn't.

Because he was a man who didn't involve himself in unnecessary drama.

ॐ

Tara strode back to her chambers with purpose. As soon as she entered, she summoned a guard.

"Call King Harshat to my room," she ordered.

She waited.

The tea table was set. The scent of warm spices filled the air. She reached for her bookshelf, selecting a few books and placing them on her bed, their pages filled with knowledge and stories she would soon share.

She had made her decision. And she had a plan.

A soft knock interrupted her thoughts.

"I'm here," Harshat's voice announced from the doorway.

Tara turned, watching as he stepped inside. The golden embroidery on his tunic caught the candlelight, casting a glow around him. But it wasn't the fabric or the finery that made her pause. It was his face.

He was smiling.

Not the polite, rehearsed smile of a king, but something softer. Genuine.

For a brief moment, something in Tara's chest twisted.

Was she making the right choice?

Shaking off the thought, she walked toward him, taking his hand in hers. It was the first time she had initiated such an intimate gesture, and she felt the subtle way his breath hitched. The softness in his eyes melted with her touch, his joy evident in the way his fingers curled gently around hers.

She guided him to the chair, sitting across from him, her heart steady despite the weight of the conversation ahead.

"Harshat," she began, her voice even, "I've thought a lot about your proposal."

His grip on the armrest tightened, anticipation flickering across his face.

"I'm ready to give us a chance," she continued. "I want to try... to give the girls a better life."

His expression brightened, but then—

"But," she added, and his smile faltered slightly.

His brows drew together in curiosity. "What condition?" he asked, voice firm. "If it's within my power, I will do it."

Tara exhaled softly, looking him straight in the eye.

"It's nothing grand," she said. "I want you to spend your nights in my room. I want to read books to you until you fall asleep. Will you?"

Harshat blinked. For a second, he seemed taken aback, as if expecting something entirely different. But then, his confusion melted into something warmer.

His lips curved into a smile.

"Of course, I will," he said without hesitation. "It would be my pleasure to listen to your musical voice as I sleep."

Then, a pause. A thoughtful crease between his brows. "But... it will be uncomfortable for you, won't it? Sleeping beside a stranger?"

Relief flooded Tara. He was a good man. A respectful one.

"It will be," she admitted with a small smile. "But we'll take small steps. We don't need to—" she hesitated, her cheeks warming slightly, "sleep while cuddling or anything. Just like our first night."

She met his gaze, her expression sincere. "I know it's quite shameless of me to ask a man this, but I'm willing to give us a try."

Harshat's entire being softened.

For a fleeting moment, he wanted to pull her into his arms, to hold her close and let her feel the depth of his emotions. But he knew better. Small steps. That was the key.

They would build something real.

Not for a kingdom. Not for duty.

But for themselves.

☙

Two Weeks of Falling

The days passed, weaving them closer.

Their bond deepened—not just in the fleeting touches that lingered longer than necessary, not just in the way their eyes sought each other in a crowded room, but in the laughter, the teasing, the effortless way they understood each other.

Tara found herself drawn to Harshat in ways she hadn't anticipated. It was no longer about duty, about obligation.

It was about *him.*

Harshat, too, realized something profound—his feelings for her had nothing to do with the girl in the painting.

It was *Tara* he was falling for.

Not an image. Not a ghost from the past.

Her.

The woman who challenged him. The woman who matched him in wit, in fire, in strength.

And just when it seemed like the universe was aligning them in the most unexpected of ways—

౹౩

The morning sun spilled through the windows, bathing the palace in golden light. But within the walls of Tara's chamber, something was wrong.

She swayed on her feet.

The world tilted.

And then—darkness.

By the time her consciousness returned, hushed whispers filled the room. Blurred figures surrounded her, their voices tinged with concern.

Amba. Kashi. The other queens.

And Harshat.

His hand clasped hers tightly, his thumb tracing soft circles against her skin. His face hovered close, his usual composed demeanor cracked with worry.

The doctor, an elderly woman with years of experience, finished her examination. A slow, knowing smile crept onto her lips as she straightened.

Then, she turned to the crowd.

"Congratulations!" she announced, her voice bursting with joy.

The room fell into stunned silence.

Harshat's grip tightened around Tara's hand. His heart pounded against his ribs.

"The state is going to have an heir soon!" the doctor declared, laughter bubbling in her chest. "King Harshat, distribute sweets!"

Laughter. Gasps. Tears.

Tara lay still, the realization crashing over her like a tidal wave.

She was pregnant.

Harshat's breath left him in a rush. He looked at Tara, searching her face, his own overcome with emotion.

Tara, his Tara, was carrying *his* child. False.

The room erupted into celebration, yet for the two of them—
Everything had changed.

The moment Tara's eyelids fluttered open, a chorus of joyous voices erupted around her.

"Rani Tara, congratulations!"

One of the senior servants rushed to her bedside, grasping her hands with warm reverence. Before Tara could even process her surroundings, she found herself being gently guided out of her room, her feet moving instinctively.

As she stepped into the grand hall, her breath hitched.

The sight before her was nothing short of mesmerizing. Every corner of the room was adorned with fresh flowers, their fragrance weaving through the air in delicate tendrils. Ornate decorations gleamed under the golden light of the chandeliers, casting a soft, ethereal glow over the gathered queens.

At the center of it all stood a throne—grand, extravagant, and adorned more lavishly than anything else in the room.

Harshat stood just behind it, his usual stoic expression softened by a rare, unguarded warmth.

And then, in a sight she had never expected—

The Father King.

Smiling.

For the first time.

Tara was led toward the throne, her movements slow, hesitant. The moment she took her seat, a ripple of celebration spread through the room. One by one, the other queens approached her, draping her in delicate floral jewelry. Heavy gold ornaments were nowhere to be seen—by the Father King's own decree, no unnecessary weight would be placed upon her.

Music filled the air, the rhythmic beats of drums blending seamlessly with the chiming laughter of the queens. Dancers twirled in elegant spirals, their skirts fanning out like blossoming flowers. Joy overflowed, spilling into every corner of the palace.

Yet amidst the revelry, a shadow crept into Tara's heart.

She should have felt happy. She should have let herself bask in this moment.

But she couldn't.

Her chest ached with the weight of a truth she could not yet reveal.

A presence settled beside her.

The Grand Queen.

Without a word, she picked up a piece of sweet and held it to Tara's lips. A silent offering, a quiet acknowledgment. Tara accepted it, her fingers brushing against the elder queen's hand.

A faint, wistful smile played on the Grand Queen's lips.

"I hope he only becomes yours."

Tara stilled. The words, though soft, carried the weight of years of heartbreak.

But something had changed. The grief, the bitterness, the simmering rage—it was all gone.

What remained was determination. Steady. Unshakable.

Tara's throat tightened.

"I'm sorry... I took away your love—"

The Grand Queen's voice faltered as Tara gently placed another sweet in her mouth, cutting her off.

"Don't," Tara murmured. "It's your special day too. Let's talk about this later."

The older woman swallowed hard, then nodded.

One by one, the other queens came forward, offering their congratulations. Even Rani Bela, too frail to walk alone, was carried to the gathering. Tara took her into her arms, letting her rest beside her on the ornate *jhula* (swing), her small frame light as a feather.

Then—

Harshat.

He approached her with a smile, the corners of his eyes crinkling slightly as he reached for a sweet.

"Congratulations," he murmured, pressing a piece of the sugary delight against her lips.

She accepted it, nodding slightly.

"Let's do this," he said.

Tara met his gaze and nodded again, firmer this time.

Then came the Father King.

His laughter boomed across the hall as he clapped his hands together.

"Ahh, I am so happy today! After so many years, an heir is finally coming into my home! Hahahaha!"

His joy was boundless, his pride evident in the way he commanded a servant forward.

A large golden key was placed into his outstretched palm.

"This," he declared, holding it up for all to see, "is the key to the treasure house of the late Mother Queen. And now, I entrust it to you."

His voice carried an unmistakable finality, a sense of passing down power.

But Tara didn't reach for the key.

"Father," she said, her voice careful yet firm. "I don't want this. But I do have a request—may I ask for something else?"

The Father King blinked.

Then, he let out a booming laugh.

"Take the key, Putri! Keep it! And still, I will grant your other wishes. You have given me the most pleasant news today!"

Power still dripped from his voice, a subtle reminder that even though Harshat wore the crown, the true authority remained with him.

Tara didn't hesitate.

"I want all of us to go on a trip," she said quickly. "We'll announce the news to the public soon anyway. Let us have a joyful moment before that."

The Father King hesitated, his brow furrowing as he considered.

Harshat stepped in, adding, "She won't be able to travel after a few months. It is best to go now."

A long silence stretched between them.

Then—finally—

"Fine," the Father King relented.

$$\text{❧}$$

A Plan in Motion

"Manchitrana!"

The word rang out like a joyous proclamation.

All the queens huddled around the map, their voices overlapping in heated debate. After endless deliberation, their final decision had been made.

Tara leaned back slightly, watching them with quiet amusement.

Suddenly—

"Tara, what is the size of the baby right now?"

The innocent question made her chuckle.

"Right now? Almost nonexistent," she teased.

A collective gasp.

"Nonexistent?! Then how did the doctor know there's a baby inside you?"

Tara fought back laughter.

"She can talk to it," she said conspiratorially. "Through her knowledge."

A dramatic pause. She pointed to her face, pulling a mock-serious expression.

The younger queens gasped in awe.

"Wow! She is so talented!"

"But how will the baby grow?"

Tara reached over, playfully pinching Sudeshna's cheek.

"The baby eats what I eat. That's how it grows."

Sudeshna frowned.

"But what if the baby wants laddoo and you eat kheer?"

A burst of laughter escaped Tara before she could stop it.

Rani Vaishali and Rudraveena, the eldest among them, simply sat back, enjoying the chaos.

ಜ

Amidst the laughter, Tara caught the eye of one of her trusted servants.

Subtly, she gestured for her to come closer.

A small, folded note slipped into the servant's hand.

"Deliver this to the Father King," Tara whispered. "Do not go through anyone else. Hand it to him yourself."

The servant nodded and slipped away.

ಜ

The Father King's chambers were bustling with attendants, his good mood evident in the way he laughed freely.

The guard stepped forward.

"Your Highness, Rani Tara has sent a message for you."

The Father King, still riding the high of victory, waved his hand.

"Let the messenger in!"

The servant entered, bowed deeply, and placed the letter on his table before silently exiting.

The Father King, still smiling, unfolded the parchment.

His eyes moved across the page.

And then—

The smile vanished.

His fingers clenched around the paper.

His jaw tightened.

The words stared back at him, sharp as daggers.

"Dear Father King, Please help me kill all of the queens..."

Just then, Bela's joyful giggle cut through the tension. The moment shifted as the child laughed at some joke only she understood. Tara found herself laughing softly, her heart lightening for a moment.

The emotional moment passed as the conversation turned back to the lighthearted. Tara's mind, however, remained focused on the purpose of this journey—the reason she had asked for it.

"Please, stop the carriage!" Tara's voice rang out unexpectedly, breaking the flow of their laughter.

Kashi's brow furrowed in concern. "What's wrong?"

Tara's face was pale, and her voice quiet. "I'm not feeling well. Let's rest here for a moment. I'll be fine after some time."

Kashi, ever the caretaker, gently guided her to a large stone under the shade of a tree. "Alright, take some rest. You'll feel better soon."

As Tara settled down, Bela added her own trademark comment, which seemed to lighten the mood once again. "Uwahhwe!"

Moments later, Harshat's presence was felt as he approached, dismounting his horse. He moved toward them, his face etched with concern.

"Why did you stop?" His voice held a hint of worry as he knelt beside Tara.

Kashi quickly explained. "Tara got tired and wanted some fresh air. She'll feel better after a little rest."

Bela added her own insight, nodding earnestly as though her opinion was vital to the conversation.

Harshat, though weary from the journey, didn't argue. He simply gave an understanding nod. "Alright then. I'll take the others to the camp we set up and come back to get you both."

The words weren't spoken to Tara but rather to the soldiers, giving them their next set of orders. As he turned to walk away, Bela's hand reached out, pinching him near the ankle.

"Ouch! You rasc—"

He cut himself off abruptly, noticing the glares from both Tara and Kashi. He cleared his throat awkwardly, his voice softening. "Ahem. Excuse me."

With that, he quickly made his exit, leaving half the soldiers behind to ensure Tara's safety.

The plan was simple: Harshat would escort the other queens and soldiers to their destination, while Tara, Kashi, and Bela would rest in a temporary tent. Once they were settled, Harshat would return alone to escort the remaining queens.

As the hours passed, the women spent their time chatting and laughing, reminiscing about childhood memories. Kashi shared a story about pushing Harshat into a pond when they were young, and Tara recalled the time she had brought flowers to her sister. Their laughter rang through the air, a stark contrast to the heaviness that lay beneath their words.

Finally, Harshat returned, his expression tired but relieved to see them.

"At last, you're here!" Kashi remarked, half-frustrated, half-amused, no doubt remembering Bela's odd habit of trying to eat dirt.

Harshat sighed, his exhaustion visible. "I've arranged for the others to set up camp. Two of them will stay behind. We need to move—let's get going."

Tara, noticing his weariness, smiled kindly. "Leave the horse to the others. Come, sit with us in the carriage. It's been a long journey for you too."

Kashi, ever considerate, added, "Yes, take a rest while we go. You can get a proper one when we reach our destination."

Harshat, with a reluctant nod, agreed. "I'll take your suggestions."

With some help, he climbed into the carriage, joining Kashi and Tara. As the carriage began to move, Harshat leaned back, closing his eyes.

The journey continued, the tension building with each passing moment. When they finally arrived at their destination, a horrible sight awaited them.

The flames of a raging fire danced in the distance, and the smell of smoke filled the air. Their eyes widened as they saw what had been destroyed.

"Maharaj, Maharani, the other queens... they're no more." The words from the messenger struck like a cold wind. "We tried to save them, but we couldn't."

Harshat and Tara exchanged a look.

"*Good*," they both said in unison, their voices cold, detached.

Kashi stared at them, her heart heavy with fear and confusion. She could hardly believe her ears. What had just happened?

Kashi's eyes were wide, filled with disbelief and fear as she stumbled forward, clutching Bela tightly to her chest. "What do you mean, *good*?! There's still time! We can save them—please, Maharaj, do something!" Her voice cracked, the panic in it as raw as the desperation in her heart. She couldn't breathe, couldn't think—her mind was clouded by the thought of those she had once called sisters, now possibly lost forever.

Tara moved swiftly to her side, her hand gently guiding Kashi to stillness as she took Bela from her arms. "Calm down, didi," she said softly, her voice a soothing whisper against the tension that crackled in the air. "There's nothing to worry about."

But Kashi's heart refused to listen. "Calm down?!" she cried, her voice rising in pitch. "Tara, they're *my family*—they may be my sautan, but I love them! How can you say there's nothing to worry about?!" The words tumbled out like stones, heavy and desperate.

Tara reached out to Harshat, offering him Bela. "Hold her," she urged, knowing the cold distance he maintained from Kashi. He looked at her, his face tightening with discomfort. "What? I—I'm not holding her." His fear was palpable, his hands stiff with hesitation.

"Don't hold the baby then, just **hold your wife**," Tara said, her voice gentle but firm. Kashi needed support, and if Harshat couldn't do that for her, he could at least offer her some comfort. Reluctantly, Harshat wrapped his arms around Bela, a low growl escaping his lips. The tiny girl slapped him across the face with an indignation that made Tara smile, despite the heavy mood.

"Let's go," Tara urged softly, guiding Kashi to a nearby tent where the other girls had been gathered for safety. Harshat trailed behind, clearly unsettled by the tension between him and Kashi. Bela, with a surprising amount of strength for such a small child, pinched his lips as they walked, reminding him of their earlier encounter.

As they entered the tent, Kashi was greeted by a chorus of youthful voices. "Maharani!" The girls rushed to her side, their faces alight with joy, undeterred by the situation that had sent them fleeing. They enveloped Kashi in a flurry of hugs, their small hands clinging to her as if their warmth could heal her pain.

"Don't worry, grand queen, we're all safe!" One of the girls spoke, her voice full of reassurance. Her words were like a balm to Kashi's frantic heart. She pulled them close, kissing each of their foreheads, her tears flowing freely now—tears of relief, of love. Her world felt steady again, the panic receding as she confirmed that they were indeed safe.

When she finally turned to Tara and Harshat, her questions were sharp. "Then why did they say... and what about the burned house?" Her voice wavered with uncertainty. She couldn't fathom the meaning behind what she had been told earlier.

One of the girls quickly guided Kashi to a seat, making sure she was comfortable. "Sit down, didi. And Tara didi too, the baby must be tired as well," she said kindly. Tara smiled at the girl's thoughtfulness, acknowledging the tender care they were receiving.

Harshat, on the other hand, took his place in a nearby chair, his face shadowed with thoughts of his own. Bela, in his arms, was nearly asleep, a quiet peace falling over her after the chaos they had experienced.

Kashi wiped her eyes dry, her face a mixture of confusion and concern. "Now, tell me what's going on," she said, her voice unsteady but determined to understand. Tara's sigh was barely audible as she gathered her thoughts, preparing to tell the truth at last.

"I'm sorry I didn't tell you before, or any of the other girls," Tara began, her tone regretful but resolute. "It could have been a disaster if it had leaked out too soon, but now I have to tell you. The father king knew of my pregnancy, but I sent him two separate letters—one in case the first one was discovered. In it, I made a request, and Harshat and I agreed on a plan together."

Kashi's brow furrowed as she listened intently. "What kind of plan?" she asked, her voice edging on urgency.

Tara took a deep breath. "We asked the king to stage an arson, to fake the deaths of all 19 queens. It would be a dramatic act—everyone in the world would believe the queens had perished in the flames. But the truth is, no one knows the face of the 19 queens. In court, only the grand queen is ever presented. So, when the news spread that they were dead, we planned to return with rescued girls—daughters of sages, adopted by the father king in honor of those lost queens."

She paused, looking at the girls gathered around them. "These girls can now have the life they deserve. They will be raised in wealth and security, not in poverty. And when the time comes, they can choose their own futures, even marry other princes if they wish."

Kashi's eyes widened as the full weight of Tara's words sank in. "That's brilliant," she whispered, her voice filled with admiration. "They'll have a life they never could have dreamed of. A life of dignity." She turned to the girls, smiling through her tears. "You'll finally be free."

Tara nodded, but there was a quiet ache in her heart. Kashi's next question pierced through her thoughts. "But what about you?" One of them asked, her voice barely above a whisper. "What about you three? What happens to you?"

Tara's gaze flickered toward Harshat, who had settled into the chair, looking weary but resolute. "We'll figure it out," Tara said softly, her voice steady despite the tangled emotions swirling within her. "We'll be fine. You don't need to worry about us."

Harshat stood, cradling the sleeping Bela in his arms. "It's late," he said, his tone quiet but final. "Let's go to sleep. Tomorrow's another day." He glanced at Kashi and Tara, his eyes softening with a rare gentleness. "We'll make it through this."

Kashi nodded, wiping away the last of her tears. The girls settled into their beds, their exhaustion finally catching up with them. Tara and Kashi followed suit, each retreating to their own resting place, the world outside momentarily forgotten.

As the night settled over them, a sense of quiet resolve filled the tent. They were not yet free of their struggles, but they would face them together. And for the moment, that was enough.

XXVI

The morning light broke through the sky, warm and fresh, a new day offering the promise of peace. Tara and Harshat, in their quiet escape, decided to take a stroll outside, their true identities hidden beneath humble clothes. Harshat donned a simple beige tunic, a quiet contrast to his usual regal attire, and Tara chose a modest saree, the rich fabric soft against her skin, complemented by a delicate necklace of dried tulsi branches. "I'm ready, let's go," Harshat said, his voice calm yet carrying an air of anticipation. Tara gave him a quiet nod, her eyes twinkling with something unspoken.

They wandered through the bustling marketplace, where vibrant colors and lively sounds painted a picture of a world untouched by the weight of their titles. Tara, ever curious, stopped by a group performing an entertainment skit. The actors moved gracefully, captivating the crowd. As she watched, something unexpected happened—Harshat's hand brushed lightly against the back of her neck. At first, Tara's body stiffened, nerves prickling with the unfamiliar sensation. But then, the warmth of his touch spread across her skin, and she allowed herself to relax into it, a shiver of anticipation running through her. His fingers glided over her collarbones, sweeping her hair to the side with a tenderness that felt almost too intimate in the public space.

The gentle caress lingered as his hand moved up to her earlobe, brushing the sensitive skin there. Tara's breath caught in her throat, a tremor passing through her. She couldn't suppress the small gasp that escaped her as he tucked a white rose into her hair. The flower, pure and fragile, felt like it belonged there, but it was the way Harshat had placed it, with such reverence and care, that sent an electric thrill through her.

"The flower is able to show its beauty because of you," he whispered, his voice low and hushed against the background noise of the crowd. "It should be arrogant to know it was kept in your hair." His words lingered in her ear, and even the heat of his breath felt like an intoxicating promise, making her heart race faster. Tara smiled shyly, her cheeks flushed with an emotion she couldn't quite name. "Thank you," she managed, her voice soft, as if afraid to disturb the delicate bubble between them.

The connection remained unbroken as Harshat gently held her hand, never letting go. The simple act of their hands intertwined, their fingers wrapped around one another, was enough to make Tara feel something stir within her—something that could no longer be ignored.

After the skit, they wandered further into the market, where the air was thick with the scent of sweets. Tara's eyes lit up as she gazed at the beautifully crafted treats displayed in the window of a sweet shop. "Look at all these sweets," she marveled, a soft smile playing at the corners of her lips. "So beautifully crafted."

Harshat, ever playful, pointed at a unique animal-shaped sweet that caught his eye. "How much is this?" he asked the shopkeeper, his voice casual. But before the shopkeeper could answer, Harshat acted swiftly—his hand snatching two of the sweets before he grabbed Tara's hand and dashed off. Tara barely had time to process what had happened. "What are you doing?" she asked, breathless, confusion lining her face as they ran, the sound of shouts echoing behind them.

"Thief! Thief!" The cry rang out in the distance, and Tara's heart raced. "Did you steal something?" she asked, the shock clear in her voice, her breath quick and panicked.

Harshat's smile never faltered as he looked back at her. "Don't worry, priye," he said, his voice light with amusement. "I put a gold coin in the basket before running." He let out a long, satisfied sigh, as though proud of his little act. Tara's eyes widened in disbelief. "Then why were we running?" she demanded, her voice rising in frustration.

"Just for fun," he replied with a laugh, his joy infectious. Tara huffed, exasperated, but there was a warmth in her chest, a fluttering sensation that had nothing to do with the running and everything to do with the way his presence made everything feel lighthearted and carefree.

Rain began to fall just as they took shelter under a tree, the soft patter of droplets turning into a steady downpour. Tara looked up at the sky, her face a mixture of amusement and challenge. "Now what?" she teased, echoing Harshat's earlier words with a playful smile.

"Now what?" Harshat repeated, frustration tinging his tone. He threw his arms up in mock defeat.

With a mischievous grin, Tara pulled him by the hands, dragging him out of the shelter and into the rain. "Tara! What are you doing?!" Harshat exclaimed, his voice a mix of laughter and disbelief. "We'll get sick!"

Tara closed her eyes, smiling as the rain soaked her completely. "Just for fun," she whispered, mimicking his voice from earlier. She laughed at the expression on his face, teasing him further. "I didn't know King Harshat was so weak that he'd get a fever from playing in the rain."

His pride flared, and with a laugh of his own, he stepped forward, his arms outstretched. "Of course not! Bring it on!" he shouted, his defiance clear.

The rain fell in torrents, soaking them both, their clothes clinging to their bodies, hair heavy and limp with water. Tara slipped slightly on the slick ground, and Harshat caught her instantly, his grip firm around her waist. They froze in that moment, the world falling away as they locked eyes. In the stillness of the rain, it felt like time had stopped, the weight of their emotions hanging in the air between them. The unspoken words, the silent yearning, were there, but neither could bring themselves to say it.

Harshat's hand moved gently, pushing Tara's pallu to cover her face, a delicate gesture that felt intimate and tender. Their breaths came in shallow, synchronized bursts as they stood so close that their lips nearly touched, the distance between them impossibly small. Tara's heart pounded, each second stretching into eternity. But just as their lips were a breath away, something pulled her back—something darker, heavier. Guilt.

The sudden wave of guilt overwhelmed her—guilt for the love she was beginning to feel, for the way she was allowing herself to be swept away by Harshat's affection. He was Kashi's. She was just a replacement, a shadow in a love that didn't belong to her. She was betraying Kashi, even if Harshat's heart whispered otherwise. The thought was unbearable.

"Let's go home," she whispered, her voice breaking the tension. Their lips brushed together ever so lightly as she spoke the words. Harshat's smile softened, unaware of the turmoil in her heart. "Let's go," he said, his tone warm and carefree, as if the world was as simple as the two of them.

He helped her stand, gently removing her pallu and placing it back with care. Though their bodies were still drenched, the rain had slowed, leaving them a little drier, the air thick with the weight of everything unsaid.

They walked back toward the tent, side by side, but with a distance between their hearts that neither of them could yet bridge. Harshat reached for her hand, but Tara hesitated for a moment before allowing it. Her heart longed to hold on, but her mind screamed that this wasn't hers to claim. She should help Kashi, restore what had been lost, and walk away from the storm that raged inside her. But for now, she stayed. For now, she held on.

XXVII

The sun hung low in the sky as the day drew to a close, signaling the end of one chapter and the beginning of another. The girls—now dressed simply to maintain their humble disguise—were escorted through the grand gates of the palace, greeted with a cascade of flowers. The civilians, unaware of the truth behind the elaborate charade, showered them with petals, their faces beaming with joy at the arrival of the "new princesses" of the kingdom.

The procession continued, each girl stepping forward, one by one, to touch the father king's feet and receive his blessings. His words were kind, though a weight hung over them. *"Stay happy, dears,"* he murmured as he offered his blessing. When the letters first arrived advising him to carry out such a horrific act—to set fire to his queens, to allow the world to believe they had perished—he was caught off guard, confused. But then, Tara's letter had explained everything. It had been a calculated gamble to secure the future of the unborn heir, a dark pact he had reluctantly agreed to.

The girls, now hidden behind their new identities as princesses, were led into the palace. Inside, the air was thick with the excitement of their arrival, but among the bustle, Bela—still shaken by the chaos—clung to Vaishali, her small form trembling.

Once the event was over and the girls had been designated to their rooms, Kashi retreated to her own quarters. She instructed a servant to take care of Bela, as was the usual routine, and settled into a familiar solitude.

Tara, however, was lost in her thoughts. The weight of what had transpired—her choices, her sacrifice—seemed to hang on her like an invisible cloak, and she could not shed it, not even for a moment. Harshat, ever close, continued his subtle gestures of affection, but Tara's response was distant, almost cold. It did not escape his notice, but he kept silent, knowing that such conversations were better suited for private moments.

As the day wound down and the evening crept in, they found themselves in Tara's room. The usual ritual of reading was meant to begin, but something was different tonight. Tara, her eyes downcast, let out a long sigh. "Harshat, I'm tired tonight. I can't read. Let's just go to sleep."

His brows furrowed, the unspoken question pressing at the back of his mind. He sat beside her, his voice steady, yet laced with concern. "Okay, no reading. But we need to talk. Why are you ignoring me?"

Her heart clenched, the words bubbling up, yet she forced them down. She couldn't say it, couldn't let him see the crack in her resolve. She had made this choice, and it was for the greater good, wasn't it? "I'm not ignoring you, I'm just... tired."

Harshat's patience was thinning, and he leaned forward, his gaze intent on hers. "No, Tara. This isn't about being tired. Why are you pulling away from me?" His voice softened, his hand reaching for hers, pleading without words.

Tara's heart ached at the sight, but she could not allow herself to fall further into his orbit. Not now. Not when it would hurt them both more in the end. She took a breath, steadying herself before she spoke again. "Promise me something," she said, her voice barely above a whisper.

Harshat paused, his brow knitting in confusion. "What?"

She held out her hand, a symbol of the promise she wanted to make, though it felt like an unspoken ultimatum. "Promise me you will love Kashi."

The words hit him like a slap. His eyes searched hers, disbelief washing over him. "What are you saying? I've already told you—"

"That you don't see her as a woman," Tara interrupted, her voice breaking slightly. "I know. But she loves you. She does."

Harshat recoiled, his frustration bubbling to the surface. "Loves me? What am I supposed to do with that? Should I be grateful to her for that?" His tone was sharper now, the simmering anger evident.

Tara's own emotions flared, her voice rising in response. "Yes, you should! Do you know how much pain she went through just to get your affection?!" She stood now, her hands clenched in fists at her sides.

She continued, her words cutting deeper with every syllable. "You should be thankful. You should accept her. Her life has been ruined because you couldn't find the courage to stand up."

Harshat's temper snapped. He grabbed something from the table and hurled it across the room, his voice laced with fury. "Yes, it was my fault, but why are you punishing my love for you? Why punish us?!" His chest heaved with anger, his hands trembling with the force of his emotions.

"Because punishing you can only be done by punishing your love," Tara whispered, tears streaming down her face. Her heart was breaking, but it was the only way she knew how to handle this—the only way she could reconcile what she had done.

Harshat stepped forward, his eyes burning with desperation. "And what about us, Tara? What about the love you have for me? Why are you doing this to us?" He reached for her shoulders, gripping them tightly. "I just want to be yours, Tara. Please."

Tara broke free from his grasp, her voice shaking as she looked up at him, her words fractured and painful. "We got married, yes. We fell in love, yes. And maybe... maybe we'll have a child one day. But the truth is... I can never be just yours. And you can never be just mine."

Harshat's heart shattered at her words. The pain in his chest was unbearable, a heavy weight he couldn't lift. He grabbed her arms once more, his voice raw, pleading. "Then why do you still love me? Why are you sacrificing our love for someone else?"

Tara's eyes filled with sorrow. "Because I can't live with the guilt of taking someone else's love away. Kashi... she deserves you. She's like a sister to me. I can't... I can't do this to her."

Her words rang in the silence between them. They stood there, both broken in different ways, yearning to close the distance between them, to make things right, but knowing that they could never return to where they once were.

Harshat, exhausted and defeated, left the room without another word, the door clicking shut behind him.

Tara collapsed onto the bed, her sobs quiet but endless. It was as if the universe itself had conspired to make her first love both beautiful and devastating. She had fallen for Harshat, but now she had to let him go—because love, it seemed, could never be purely hers to keep. She had to kill her love with her own hands, for the sake of someone else's happiness.

Outside the door, Kashi overheard the argument, the pain in Tara's voice unmistakable. Her heart shattered as she processed the reality of what had just happened. Tara, the woman she had loved like a sister, had sacrificed her own happiness for her. But Kashi knew what she had to do now. Love could never be forced—it had to be given freely, without guilt. She would find a way to fix this. She would make sure that Tara and Harshat's love was not lost to sacrifice.

Elsewhere in the palace, two shadowy figures moved silently through the halls. Their faces hidden, their intentions unclear, they lingered in the darkness, watching, waiting for the right moment.

XXVIII

The morning unfolded like a dream in slow motion, the hours passing by without real meaning. Tara sat by the window, staring out into the vast expanse of the kingdom, but her mind refused to leave the shadows of last night. The argument, the painful words exchanged with Harshat, echoed relentlessly in her mind, each one like a shard of glass slicing through her thoughts. How she wished Nayna were here, her sister, her constant support, to guide her through this storm. But Nayna was far away, still on her journey, leaving Tara to navigate the chaos alone.

Tara knew she could not remain in this fragile state. She had vowed to the Queen of Nazabgar that she would never be weak, never falter, not after the haunting memories of her childhood, when weakness meant survival was uncertain. Her heart trembled at the thought of the void left by Nayna's absence, but she had to move forward. The king and queen were here, just a day's ride away. She could make the journey on her own. She would.

Determined, Tara wrapped her face with a cloth to conceal her identity and slipped out of the palace, blending into the bustling market outside. The world moved around her, unaware of the royal figure in their midst. She rented a horse, feeling the tension in her body dissolve slightly as the rhythmic trot of hooves took her away from the confusion of the palace. The unfamiliar landscape soon transformed into the comforting sights of her past—the market where she and Nayna used to play, the royal gate that once stood as a symbol of freedom and confinement, both at once.

When she reached the gates of Nazabgar, the gatekeeper's voice called from above, demanding her identity. With a smile that felt foreign to her lips, Tara lowered the cloth, her voice steady despite the whirlwind inside her. "I am Tara, princess of Nazabgar and queen of King Harshat."

The gatekeeper's eyes widened, his face flushed with the shock of recognition. "Princess! I'm so sorry, I didn't recognize you at first! Open the gates! Open the gates!" His orders were shouted, and soon enough, the heavy doors creaked open, the sight of them filling Tara with a brief sense of peace. She had made it.

Soldiers rushed toward her, offering to take the horse from her, but it was Shagun, the elder soldier, who stepped forward. His eyes, warm with familiarity, met hers. "It's been so long, Princess. How are you? And how is Princess Nayna? We've heard nothing for so long."

Tara's heart swelled with the affection she had once known so intimately. "Nayna and I are both fine, Shagun Kaka. Thank you for asking, but please take care of yourself as well."

Shagun's face softened, his smile broadening. "You remember my name, Princess?" he asked, his voice tinged with surprise and pride.

"Of course I do," Tara replied, a small chuckle escaping her lips as she touched his feet in respect. "You were the one who helped us sneak out when we were children. We never forgot you, even when we stopped those little adventures."

A wave of nostalgia washed over both of them, and for a brief moment, they were not the princess and the soldier, but two old friends reminiscing about days long gone. Tara bid him farewell and moved on, the weight in her heart lifting ever so slightly as she walked deeper into the palace.

The outer walls of the palace, once a fortress of childhood games and dreams, seemed to whisper memories into her ears as she moved through the halls. The corridors, where she and Nayna used to race through the halls, the garden where they made crowns of wildflowers for each other—every corner held a fragment of her past. The kitchen, with its sweet aromas and stolen candies, the pujaghar where they prayed for a never-ending supply of sweets, the balcony where they set up their tea parties, pretending to rule the kingdom when no one else was around. And finally, the inner palace, where she knew her parents spent their hours.

The moment she entered the inner chambers, she was surrounded by the servants, each one offering their greetings, their questions tumbling out in rapid succession. "Princess, how are you?" "Why are you here alone?" "Is Princess Nayna with you?" "I heard about the queens. Are you unharmed?" The flood of inquiries overwhelmed her, and she held up a hand to calm them.

"Relax," she said with a tired smile. "I'm fine, Nayna is fine, and I can't answer the rest. Please, go get some rest. I'll speak to the king and queen."

One of the servants, Madubala, insisted on calling the royal couple immediately, but Tara gently stopped her. "No, I'll go to them. I need to speak with them alone. It's important."

The servants offered their well-wishes, and Tara made her way to the king and queen's chambers. The guards didn't question her; they simply nodded and let her pass, though she could see the surprise in their eyes. She appreciated their understanding, not wanting to engage in small talk when her heart was so heavy with the questions burning inside her.

As she entered the office, her voice rang out with the warmth of familiarity. "Maa! Baba!" The sight of her parents, sitting at their desks, working in quiet harmony, was both a comfort and a shock. They looked up, their faces frozen for a heartbeat, as if unsure whether they were seeing an illusion. Tara smiled, waving her hand in front of them. "Maa? Baba?"

It took a moment, but then they were on their feet, engulfing her in their arms. The world seemed to pause, and Tara's heart, so heavy just moments before, lightened at the embrace. "Oh my god, Tara!" Rukmini exclaimed, her voice choked with emotion. "What a pleasant surprise! How did you get here?"

Tara pulled back just enough to tease her father, "What? Not happy to see me?"

Darshan, always the joker, gave her a sheepish smile. "Of course we are, come sit down!" he said, ushering her to the long sofa.

But soon enough, the inevitable questions came. Rukmini's voice softened with concern. "How are you, my dear? And when is Nayna coming back?"

Tara hesitated, looking down. "I don't know when exactly. She replied to my letter saying she would return, but she didn't say when."

The room fell silent, heavy with unspoken words, until Rukmini spoke again, her voice gentle but insistent. "Tara, something is troubling you. What is it?"

Tara's voice trembled as she started, the words spilling out in a rush. "Maa, do you remember the time we went to Mrigpara?" Her mother nodded, waiting for her to continue. "That day, you asked Nayna to sleep, but she snuck out to see the fair. I stayed in her bed to cover for her. There, she met a boy. That boy... he was King Harshat."

The words hit her parents like a thunderclap, and Tara could see their faces change as the memories flooded back. "That boy," Tara continued, "he fell in love with Nayna. He still loves her. That's why he wanted to marry her."

Darshan pulled her into a hug, but Rukmini remained calm, her gaze steady. "Tara, you remember it wrong," she said softly, as if peeling away layers of a painful truth. "There's more to that story than you know."

Tara sat up straighter, her heart pounding. "What do you mean?"

Rukmini took a deep breath before she spoke. "When you were younger, your biological parents—my sister and her husband—used you to sell secrets to our enemies. When they were about to be caught, your father tried to kill you. He struck you on the head, but we got there just in time."

Tara's breath caught in her throat as Rukmini continued. "That blow to your head messed with your memory. That's why you sometimes confuse things. That day with Nayna, when she played with that boy, you didn't know who he really was. It was you, you went with Maharaj only as Nayna was sick"

Tara's mind raced, the pieces of the puzzle falling into place. "Then why does he have a painting of Nayna?"

Rukmini's lips curled into a sad smile. "In fear that you'd be caught, you gave him Nayna's portrait. We know this because Shagun told us. He used to follow you two around, secretly protecting you."

Tara was still processing this new information when she finally found her voice. "Maa, Baba, there's one more thing I need to ask…"

Her father placed a gentle hand on her head. "Ask away, beta."

Tara swallowed hard, her throat tight with emotion. "Kashi loves Harshat. I also love Harshat. What should I do?"

Rukmini looked down for a moment, her smile soft but understanding. Then she met Tara's gaze, her words wise and steady. "Beta, I will never tell you to take someone's love away. But you've suffered enough, and from what you've told me, Harshat loves you too. Have a conversation with him and Kashi. Then, you can decide what's best."

Tara nodded, feeling a flicker of hope, of clarity, for the first time in what felt like forever.

Just as they were about to embrace again, a faint sound broke the moment. The sharp twang of arrows cut through the air. Tara turned just in time to see the arrows pierce the air and strike with deadly precision.

The sight that followed shattered her heart. Her parents' lifeless bodies collapsed to the ground.

Shock paralyzed her, her world spinning in a blur of panic and disbelief. But amidst the chaos, she caught one critical piece of information—the shooter had been caught. The soldier's words echoed in her ears, his confession unmistakable: Harshat had ordered the hit.

Tara's vision blurred as the world around her crumbled into pieces.

XXIX

Rage, sorrow, and vengeance churned in Tara's veins like a wildfire, each emotion feeding into the next until they consumed her entirely. Her blood felt thick with fury, her vision clouded by grief. The world around her seemed to blur as she stood there, staring at her parents' lifeless bodies. *This can't be real,* she thought, wishing, praying, that she could wake up from this nightmare. If only she could return to those moments before—before she entered the room and saw her parents, warm and alive, before this unimaginable devastation tore through her world.

But then, the cold truth struck her like an icy slap. This was no nightmare. This was reality. Her parents, the people who had loved her as their own, who had raised her with tenderness and care, were gone. And in their place lay a haunting emptiness she had never known.

Her mind felt like it was drowning in a fog of confusion. The only words that managed to pierce the haze were *parents, death, assassin, Harshat.* They repeated over and over in a frantic loop, but she could hardly make sense of them. Her heart ached, but something else, something darker, burned beneath that pain: an insatiable desire for revenge.

Without thinking, Tara turned and fled the room, her footsteps echoing against the stone as she ran. Voices tried to call after her, hands reaching out to stop her, but she didn't hear them. She didn't care. She had spent so many years trying to be the dutiful daughter, the one who fixed the wrongs of her past, trying to live up to the love her adoptive parents had given her. But it had all been in vain. The man she had trusted—whom she had once thought she loved—had killed the people who had given her everything.

Her heart clenched as the questions swirled in her mind. *How could he?* *Why would he?* She didn't have time to find answers. Only one thing mattered now: vengeance.

She grabbed the reins of a horse in a rush, barely taking a moment to steady herself before spurring it into a full gallop. The horse tore through the streets, the wind whipping her face, but Tara hardly noticed. The only thing she could feel was the fire of rage that consumed her, and the only thing her mind could focus on was the path ahead—the path that led to Harshat.

Tears burned down her face, but they were not tears of weakness. They were the mark of a woman whose grief had turned into something far more dangerous. *You want to take everything from me?* her heart screamed. *Then I'll take it all from you.*

As she reached the gates of Harshat's palace, she felt nothing but cold resolve. The guards barely had time to react before she passed them, her identity no longer hidden, and her emotions no longer restrained. She didn't care about anything anymore. *Not my title. Not my life. Not my love.* All that remained was this overwhelming need for justice.

She walked through the palace halls, her feet barely touching the ground as her thoughts churned. The echo of her footsteps seemed to mock her, reminding her of the weight of the decision she had already made. The weight of the loss she would never be able to undo. Her vision tunneled, the palace around her becoming nothing but a blur as she neared Harshat's chambers. There, her revenge waited.

In a frenzy, she grabbed a sword from the wall, its cold steel a welcome extension of her fury. Without a second thought, she burst into the room, the door crashing open with force.

"*Arghhhhh!*" The scream ripped from her throat, primal and raw as she swung the sword at Harshat.

Harshat, who had been lost in the pages of a book, spun around just in time, his reflexes sharp, narrowly avoiding the blade. He staggered back, eyes wide with shock. "*Tara?*" he breathed, confusion flickering across his face as he saw the madness in her eyes. "What are you doing?"

She didn't answer. Instead, she swung again, her arm wild with rage. This time, he ducked, his movements fluid, almost graceful as he tried to make sense of the chaos that had erupted.

"*Why did you kill them?*" Tara's voice cracked, each word filled with a kind of pain that twisted her insides. It was a voice she hardly recognized, alien and raw, a voice of torment and heartbreak.

"*Kill who?*" Harshat's confusion deepened, his brow furrowing as he tried to dodge her next strike.

Tara panted, her breath coming in harsh, uneven gasps. She was fighting against more than just Harshat. She was fighting against the storm inside her, the grief, the betrayal. Her limbs felt heavy, her muscles trembling from exhaustion, but her anger, her need for revenge, drove her forward.

Harshat, realizing there was no talking sense into her in this state, moved quickly, grabbing her from behind in a headlock, pulling her close to him. He held her tightly, using his free hand to pry the sword from her grasp. Her struggles were fierce, but they were weakening.

"Tara, stop," he pleaded, his voice strained. "I don't know what you're talking about. I thought everything would be fine after this, but clearly, it's just gotten worse."

His grip tightened as he carefully took the sword's metal part and struck her lightly behind the neck, just enough to make her eyes flutter. The exhaustion in her was too much, and before she could react, her body went limp, her head falling against his chest as she fainted in his arms.

For a moment, Harshat stood there, staring down at her limp form. He hadn't wanted this. He hadn't expected this. But it was too late now.

With a deep, frustrated sigh, Harshat scooped her up, carrying her gently toward the bed. He laid her down with care, his hands lingering on her shoulders as he adjusted her position. His heart twisted with confusion, with regret. *What has happened?* he wondered, his mind racing as he looked at her, vulnerable and unconscious.

There was a truth that he had not shared with her yet, something that weighed on him more than anything else: *I love you.*

He bent down and kissed her forehead gently, brushing his lips against her skin, feeling the heat of her body beneath him. "We'll talk when you wake up," he whispered, his voice thick with emotion.

He then moved to tie her hands to the bedposts with soft satin cloth, ensuring that she wouldn't be able to hurt herself once she regained consciousness. It was a precaution, knowing that the fury in her heart would still burn bright, even if she couldn't express it just yet.

Afterward, Harshat left the room in search of answers, the weight of his actions pressing heavily on him. He ordered the grand queen and servants to change Tara's clothes and tend to her while he sought to uncover the truth behind what had driven her to this madness.

But as he walked away, his mind remained on her—on the woman who had captured his heart, and whose pain now felt like his own.

Harshat sat alone in a dimly lit room, his gaze fixed on the scattered papers in front of him. His mind was a whirlwind, each thought chasing the other with no clear resolution. His chest felt tight with guilt and frustration. Kashi's response to his request had been surprising, but not in the way he expected. She hadn't once let jealousy creep into her heart—she had simply asked about Tara's well-being, her concern overshadowing everything else. And that's when it became clear to him. She had been raised to place the needs of others above her own, and in that moment, Kashi's natural instincts kicked in. No questions, no reservations.

She had cared for Tara during her unconsciousness, never leaving her side for even a moment. She was everything Harshat needed her to be and more—calm, compassionate, and reliable. But even Kashi's strength couldn't calm the storm brewing inside of him. He still didn't know the full story. The investigation into the events surrounding his parents' deaths had led him nowhere. Despite his best efforts to extract the truth, the assassin's lips remained sealed, even as he was tortured. Harshat's fingers drummed restlessly on the table as he pondered the next steps. His hunch was clear, but it felt too risky to act on without more evidence.

Suddenly, a voice sliced through his thoughts—a feminine tone that made him glance up. *"She's almost getting her senses back. Maybe I should meet her now."* A woman stepped out of the shadows, her presence commanding, though her eyes were full of uncertainty. She was followed by a man with a British accent, his posture relaxed but his eyes sharp with intent. *"I think so too. We should meet her now,"* he said, his voice betraying a sense of urgency.

Harshat's focus remained unfaltering, his thoughts still deep in the labyrinth of the investigation. "You should. Go," he replied, his voice distant, barely acknowledging their words. He knew the time would come soon for him to confront the truth, but now wasn't that time. He needed answers, and he was running out of patience.

Meanwhile, in the quiet room where Tara lay, the air was thick with silence. Kashi had remained by her side through it all, never leaving for a single moment. Tara had awoken the previous day, but her body remained pale, drained of its vitality. She was a shadow of herself—her spirit broken, her face a fragile, colorless version of the woman she had been. Kashi spoke softly, offering words of comfort, but Tara barely acknowledged her. The pain of her parents' death was too raw, and the bitterness of betrayal—of Harshat's involvement—swallowed her whole. Kashi tried to reason with her, urging her to rest, reminding her of her pregnancy, of her health, but Tara was lost in her grief, unwilling to listen. Every breath she took felt heavier, as if the weight of her sorrow was too much to bear.

And then, the door opened.

The familiar voice of Tara's sister broke through the fog of her thoughts. "**Di**?" It was soft, tentative, but it carried the weight of something more. Tara's head jerked up, and for a moment, she thought she might be dreaming. But no—there she was. Nayna. Standing in the doorway, her eyes full of concern.

"Di?" Nayna repeated, her voice trembling as she walked to Tara's side and sat where Kashi had been moments ago. She took Tara's hands gently into her own, her fingers warm against Tara's cold skin. Tara stared at her in disbelief, the weight of the moment settling over her like a blanket. She reached out, her fingers trembling as she brushed her sister's face, almost as if to reassure herself that Nayna was real. "Nayna..." she whispered, her voice hoarse and cracked from days of unspoken grief.

Nayna smiled softly, her eyes glistening with unshed tears. "I heard what happened to Maa and Baba," she said, her voice steady but her hands shaking. Tara broke down at the sound of her sister's words, her body trembling with uncontrollable sobs. The dam that had held back her tears for so long finally shattered, and she clung to Nayna, as if holding her sister would somehow make the pain more bearable. "How could Harshat do this, Nayna?" she choked, her words coming in broken gasps. "When I finally thought I was ready to live a life with him, to love him... he betrayed me so badly. Why? Why me? I've done everything I could to make things right..."

Nayna held her sister close, her heart breaking for the pain Tara was enduring. She let Tara cry, allowing her the space to release the anguish she had been holding onto for so long. Only when the sobs began to subside did she speak again, her voice calm, though heavy with truth.

"It wasn't him," Nayna said, her words quiet but firm. Tara pulled away slightly, her tear-streaked face staring at her in confusion. "What?" she breathed, the word barely audible, her breath shallow as she processed the claim.

Nayna took a deep breath, her hands clutching Tara's with renewed intensity. "Before I tell you everything," she began, her voice unwavering despite the turmoil inside her, "I want you to meet someone." She motioned toward the door, and Andrew stepped forward, his posture calm, though his eyes were filled with the same seriousness that marked Nayna's demeanor. "This is Andrew," she said, her voice holding a note of pride. "He's a good man. And Andrew, this is my sister, Tara. You should call her Bhabhi."

Andrew blinked, momentarily lost in the unfamiliar word. "Baby?" he asked, his accent heavy with confusion.

Nayna sighed softly, correcting him with a smile, "No, Bhabhi. Bha-bee." She turned back to Tara, her voice growing serious again. "Andrew and I arrived here the day Maa and Baba were killed. We were in disguise, trying to reach you first, then the others. But as we arrived, we overheard something from King Harshat's father.

He was furious. He found out about your fake pregnancy—one of your servants must have leaked it. In his anger, he decided to kill Maa and Baba as revenge. When we heard his plan, we rushed to Nazabgar. But we were too late. They were already gone..."

Nayna's voice wavered as she spoke of the tragedy, but she continued. "We stayed hidden, Andrew and I. I couldn't—" She choked on the words, her face tightening with grief. "I couldn't do anything. But after three days, we gave Harshat the information about the assassination, but kept quiet about his father's involvement. I wanted to tell you first. I wanted you to know the truth before anyone else."

Tara sat frozen, her face pale, her mind racing to process everything Nayna had just said. The pieces of the puzzle began to fall into place, but the shock of it all left her speechless, her thoughts in chaos.

"I need some time alone," Tara whispered after a long pause, her voice thin but steady. She pulled away from her sister's embrace, her hands shaking as she clutched the blanket around her.

Nayna nodded, understanding the depth of her sister's need for space. "I'll give you some time," she said gently. With a final glance, she motioned for Andrew to follow, and they quietly left the room.

Outside, Kashi broke her silence. "This is it," she said, her voice low and tinged with disgust. "This is the final stroke." She turned to Nayna and Andrew, her gaze hardening as she introduced herself. "I'm Kashi," she said with a thin smile. "The Pratham Rani of King Harshat." Her tone shifted as she continued, the words laced with a sharpness that made them all pause. "And I'll do what a Maharani should do."

With that, she turned and left, her footsteps echoing in the silence of the hall, her resolve firm and unwavering.

XXXI

The heavy knock echoed through the room, and Harshat's voice, clipped and commanding, broke the silence. "Come in." Kashi stepped inside, her presence different this time—almost tangible, as if the very air around her had changed. Harshat's eyes met hers, and for the first time, he noticed something new in the way she stood. There was a fire in her gaze, a quiet but powerful determination that commanded the space between them. He felt it—felt the weight of her presence settle over him. It was a quiet force, but one he could not ignore.

Kashi moved forward, her steps measured and confident. "Harshat," she said, her voice calm but firm, the tone unfamiliar to him. It was the first time she had addressed him by his name, without the customary title. The sound of it, simple and unadorned, seemed to cut through the tension in the air.

"We've been married for over six years now, am I correct?" She stood tall, her back straight, her eyes unwavering as she held his gaze.

Harshat blinked, momentarily thrown by the question. "Yes... why?" he asked, his voice laced with the uncertainty that came from years of trying to navigate their complicated relationship. His father had taught him to cede to authority, to allow others to lead when it came to emotional matters, and Kashi had always been the epitome of patience, never demanding anything from him. But now, in the silence that followed her question, he felt an unsettling shift.

Kashi took a slow, steady breath. "I know I love you," she said, her voice softer now, almost tender. "But you cannot return those feelings, and that's fine. Love can never be forced." Her words were like a gentle release, the acceptance of a truth she had carried for years. She looked into his eyes, and for the first time, Harshat saw something shift within her—a quiet strength, tempered by years of patience.

"I've never wanted anything from you until now," she continued, her voice steady, unyielding. "I've always done what a grand queen should do, haven't I?" Her words were a challenge, a reminder of all the unspoken sacrifices she had made in their marriage, all the ways she had placed herself aside for him, for the kingdom. Harshat's silence was all the answer she needed.

Kashi took his hand, her touch deliberate, her fingers warm against his. She held it there, placing his palm against her forehead, her eyes searching his for any sign of resistance. "If you have any respect for me," she said, her voice low but commanding, "you will give me what I want." The weight of her words hung in the air, thick with expectation. Harshat's heart raced, his mind scrambling, trying to comprehend what she was asking of him.

"Vow that you will give me the punishment you would give any other citizen," Kashi's voice was a whisper now, but it was sharp as a blade. The request was simple, but the implications were overwhelming. She was asking him to act not as her husband, but as a king. And in doing so, she was stepping into the role she had always been destined for. Harshat felt a wave of dread wash over him. He knew he could not refuse her.

His voice was tight with uncertainty, but there was no turning back now. "Alright, I will," he said, his words barely more than a whisper, a promise he wasn't sure he could keep. But he knew, in that moment, that she would hold him to it. She had already made her decision. He just didn't know yet what she would do next.

Kashi nodded, her expression unreadable. "Thank you," she said, her voice soft but firm. With that, she turned and left the room, her presence lingering in the air long after she was gone.

Meanwhile, in the room where Tara sat, the atmosphere had shifted as well. She looked different—stronger, more at peace than she had been in days. When Nayna and Andrew entered, Tara smiled at them, her face softened by the warmth of their presence. "It's you both," she said, her voice a little lighter now. "Come and sit."

Nayna settled beside her on the bed, while Andrew took the chair nearest the window. Tara looked at Andrew with gratitude. "I'm sorry for how I acted before," she said, her voice quiet but sincere. "Thank you for taking care of my sister. I truly appreciate it."

Andrew smiled, his eyes softening as he glanced at Nayna. "No need to apologize. It's a natural reaction to want to protect someone you care about," he said, his tone warm. "And Nayna is beautiful—how could I not care about her?"

Tara smiled faintly, her heart lightened by their kindness. "And I've been learning a bit of Hindi from Nayna," Andrew added, his voice light and playful. "So if you want, we can converse in Hindi."

Tara nodded, her spirits lifting slightly at the thought of this strange new connection. She glanced at Nayna, a small chuckle escaping her lips. "Nayna," she began, her voice turning serious again, "I think I owe Harshat an apology. After what happened with Maa and Baba, I... I acted in a rush, without thinking."

Nayna's lips curved into a teasing smile. "It's one of your traits, Di," she said with a soft snicker. "You don't usually get angry, but when something bad happens, you lose your mind easily." The tension in the room seemed to lift as they shared a quiet laugh, the sound of their shared bond bringing a sense of comfort.

But the moment was broken suddenly by a sharp, metallic sound—a pocket knife flying through the air. It struck the wall near the door with a solid thud. A sharp cry followed, and a servant, pale with fear, stumbled backward, her hands trembling.

"Who are you, and what are you doing here?" Andrew's voice was cold, harsh. He rose from his chair, his posture intimidating as he faced the trembling servant.

"I—I am one of the servants," the girl stammered, her eyes downcast in fear. "I brought some fruits for Rani Tara."

"We don't need them," Nayna said sharply, her voice betraying none of the softness it had once held. She could sense Andrew's temper, and she knew how volatile he could be.

Tara, standing up, walked over and grabbed Andrew's ear, twisting it sharply. "You young man," she scolded, her voice stern but laced with affection. "Why did you target her? What if you had hurt her?! Do you think you're some kind of mafia or what?"

Andrew winced, his face contorting in mock pain. "I'm sorry, baby. I'll never do it again, I promise. Please don't twist my ear anymore." He flinched again as she let go, rubbing his ear with exaggerated gestures.

Tara sighed, shaking her head in exasperation. "Where is Rani Kashi?" she asked, turning to Nayna. "I need to speak with her."

Nayna paused, collecting her thoughts. "I think she went to the east side of the palace, near the courtroom," she replied. Tara nodded, rising from the bed with renewed determination.

"You both stay here. I'll be back after meeting Rani Kashi," Tara said as she made her way toward the door.

As she walked down the corridor, she finally spotted Kashi, her figure unmistakable against the palace's grand architecture. They met in the hall, their eyes locking before either of them spoke.

"We need to talk," both of them said at the same time.

Tara nodded, and together they moved to a quiet corner, far from the prying eyes of the palace. "Rani Kashi," Tara began, her voice soft but heavy with gratitude. "Thank you so much for taking care of me. I don't know what to say, but truly... thank you."

Kashi raised a single finger to her lips, silencing Tara with a gentle but firm gesture. "Now listen to me," she said, her tone unwavering. She took Tara's hand and placed it gently on her own forehead, a gesture filled with an unspoken promise. "Whatever happens from here on out is neither your fault, nor Harshat's. I asked him to do it. And if you have any respect for me, you will lead a happy life with Harshat."

Tara's mind raced, confusion and understanding battling within her. But Kashi's words had a weight to them, a truth that settled into her heart. She nodded slowly, unsure of what exactly would happen next, but trusting Kashi's judgment.

Later, Kashi entered the father king's chamber, her expression unreadable. The old man greeted her with a casual wave, his laughter cold and sinister as he mocked Tara's misfortune. "You killed the king and queen of Nazabgar, didn't you?" Kashi asked, her voice steady but sharp.

The father king chuckled, a dark smile playing on his lips. "Yes. How dare that girl lie to me! She should pay for that." He turned away, dismissive. "Anyway, the blame will fall on Harshat, and Tara will hate him. Use that. Get close to him, and produce a real heir this time." He scoffed, turning his back to her, unaware of the danger looming.

As soon as his back was turned, Kashi's hand moved with lightning speed, a dagger appearing from the folds of her gown. She stabbed it deep into the king's chest, the blade finding its mark with terrifying precision. "I'm the grand queen," Kashi whispered coldly, twisting the blade just enough to make him grunt in pain. "This is what I should do. Punish those who hurt my people."

The king gasped, his body faltering as he tried to turn toward her. But Kashi was already stepping back, her gaze as cold as the steel in her hand. "Goodbye," she murmured, her voice steady as the life left his eyes. And just like that, the room fell into silence.

XXXII

The news of the father king's death spread like wildfire through the palace, each corridor alive with whispers and rumors. Guards, their faces pale with disbelief, stood frozen when they saw Kashi, her hands bound by chains, standing before the lifeless body of the king. There was no room for argument, no space for grief—just the cold, hard reality of her actions laid bare for all to see.

The tension in the palace was palpable, and soon, the news reached Harshat, Tara, Nayna, and Andrew. They were gathered in a private room, a place meant for calm, but now it became the arena for their shock. Harshat, who had known Kashi since childhood, couldn't believe it. "Kashi would never do such a thing!" he exclaimed, his voice filled with disbelief. The words felt foreign, like a betrayal of everything he thought he knew about her. "*Yes!*" Tara quickly added, her voice rising in defense. "*Stop slandering the Grand Queen. It's a punishable act! It's a crime!*" Her heart ached at the thought of anyone daring to accuse Kashi of such an atrocity.

Nayna and Andrew, who had only known Kashi for a few hours, exchanged glances. They couldn't make a judgment yet. But Nayna, her gaze unwavering, held on to her faith in her sister. "*If Kashi says she didn't do it, then she didn't,*" Nayna thought. Andrew, though quieter, trusted Nayna's instincts. If Nayna believed in Kashi, so would he. There was no room for doubt.

Before they could say more, another soldier entered, breathless with urgency. "*My king!*" He bowed low, his voice quivering. "*The ministry demands an immediate answer. They want a courtroom opened now.*"

Harshat waved his hand dismissively, his mind a tangled mess of emotions. "*I know. You may leave,*" he muttered, his gaze turning toward the others. He slumped back in his chair, the weight of what was to come settling on his shoulders. "*Now what?*" The question hung in the air, unanswered, as they all exchanged troubled looks. Deep down, they all knew the consequences of Kashi's actions could no longer be avoided.

The courtroom was prepared, the grand hall filled with the murmurs of ministers and officials. Harshat sat at the top, the weight of the crown heavier than ever. Tara, Nayna, and Andrew stood behind the heavy curtains, their eyes focused on the proceedings, the tension palpable. And then, there was Kashi, standing at the center, shackled and unbowed. Her posture was regal, almost defiant, as if the chains were nothing more than a temporary inconvenience. The other queens, Vaishali and Rudraveena, stood close behind the curtains, their concern for Kashi evident in the tightness of their expressions.

The prime minister's voice cut through the silence, thick with anger and judgment. "*Maharaj, Maharani killed your father and our beloved ex-king. Please, do justice and sentence this evil sinner to death at once!*" His words rang through the hall like a hammer striking an anvil. Another minister echoed the sentiment. "*Yes, my king! How dare she kill the father king?*"

Kashi stood unmoving, her face a mask of quiet resolve. The accusation hung in the air, but there was no flicker of remorse in her eyes, no sign of the guilt they expected to see. She was silent, unyielding, as if the words had no power over her.

Harshat, lost in thought, said nothing. He didn't know how to fight this. How could he defend Kashi when the court was so certain of her guilt? It was easier, he realized, to let the anger flow and hope it would pass. He needed to divert their attention, find a way to shift the conversation.

But Rudraveena, her voice rising in fury, broke the silence. "*All of them are ungrateful!*" she said, the words laced with disbelief. "*Rani Kashi did so much for the kingdom, and now they dare to call her a murderer?*"

Vaishali, standing beside her, nodded vehemently. "*Yes! She's innocent. Someone is setting her up!*" Her eyes locked onto Tara. "*Rani Tara, please, can't you do something?*" she pleaded, desperation in her voice.

Tara's gaze was fixed on Kashi, a quiet sorrow in her eyes. "*I will do what I can,*" she said softly, her voice thick with emotion. "*But now is not the time. Acting hastily will only make things worse.*" Her hands clenched at her sides, but she knew the truth—they had no choice but to let the court decide.

At last, Harshat's voice broke through the chaos. "*Rani Kashi,*" he began, the words heavy with reluctance. "*The allegation of killing the father king lies upon you. There were many guards as witnesses. What do you have to say in your defense?*" His voice trembled, though he tried to hide it, and there was an unsettling quiet in the air as every eye in the room turned to Kashi.

Kashi stood tall, her chains rattling slightly as she exhaled slowly. "*I have nothing to say, Maharaj,*" she said, her voice steady and clear, the words as sharp as steel. "*The truth is as clear as water. I killed the father king with my own hands.*" The confession fell like a stone in the silence of the room. It was not the confession they expected, nor the one they were prepared for. Kashi stood there, unflinching, her eyes calm, as though she were speaking of a trivial matter.

Harshat's mind raced, but his voice faltered. "*If so,*" he said, his tone strained, "*what was your motive behind it?*" He had to understand. Why would she admit to such a thing so easily?

Kashi's eyes flickered with something unreadable, her voice unwavering. "*I held a grudge against him,*" she said, her tone measured, as though recounting a history that had long been settled. "*He never handed full power over to me. He always kept me in the shadows, even when I was ready to lead. And he killed Rani

Tara's parents, and he wanted me to clear his name for that.*" She paused, her words cutting through the tension like a blade. "*I got frustrated. I killed him because of all of it.*"

Her voice was eerily calm, as though she had prepared this speech long ago. The words echoed in the hall, leaving a trail of shock in their wake.

Harshat's mind spun, the weight of his promise pressing down on him. Kashi had reminded him of his own vow, the one he had made before all of this chaos began. But how could he reconcile his duty with his love for her? She had confessed to the crime. His hands were tied.

"*Since the criminal has confessed to their crimes,*" the prime minister's voice rang out, cold and final. "*According to the law of our kingdom, I, King Harshat, announce the death penalty to Rani Kashi—*" He began to speak the judgment, but his words were cut off by a sudden, forceful interruption.

"*I object!!*" Tara's voice rang out, sharp and fierce, every syllable laced with indignation. She stood, her eyes blazing with determination. "*Rani Kashi would never do such a thing. And even if she did, how can we treat her so harshly after all the years of dedication she has given to this kingdom?*"

The room went silent, the weight of her words hanging in the air like a storm ready to break. The prime minister, his face reddening with fury, snapped. "*Don't act foolish, how dare you interrupt the king!*"

Tara's response was instant, a defiance that couldn't be ignored. "*I, as the second wife and second queen of the king, have every right to cut off his words!*" She stood her ground, her voice unyielding.

The prime minister's eyes narrowed, and he sneered. "*Yes, Your Majesty, but you do not have the power to impose decisions in the outer court, just as the king does not have that power in the inner palace.*"

Tara's jaw clenched, but she was left with no argument. The truth of the matter stung, and she sank back into her seat, the fire in her chest still burning but unable to manifest.

"*Silence!*" Harshat's voice, strained and authoritative, cut through the tension. "*Rani Kashi will be held captive in prison for now. After a thorough investigation, if she's found guilty, she will be executed in public. Guards, take her away.*"

The finality of his words echoed through the hall, and the court was dismissed, the weight of the judgment hanging over them all. As Kashi was led away, her head held high, she cast one last glance at Harshat, and he knew—whether or not she would be executed, she had already made

her choice. And now, it was too late to turn back.

XXXIII

The palace, though still and silent on the outside, was a storm of turmoil within. Vaishali and Rudraveena retreated to their rooms, the weight of recent events still pressing on their hearts. The ministers and courtiers returned to their duties, though their minds were clouded with whispers of the trial. Andrew, too, was given a separate room to rest, though he found little peace there. Meanwhile, Nayna chose to stay in Tara's room, her mind restless with worry for her sister, Kashi.

Tara, her thoughts unsettled, knew she needed answers—answers only Harshat could provide. The idea of Kashi facing the death penalty filled her with dread, and she couldn't shake the nagging feeling that Harshat's emotions, tangled with grief for his father, might push him toward irreversible action. She was sure of one thing: the conversation was too urgent to wait. She could no longer knock politely on his door.

Without hesitation, Tara entered Harshat's office chamber, her footsteps light but filled with intent. Harshat, absorbed in his papers, glanced up, startled by her sudden entrance. But when he saw her, he gave a subtle nod and set the papers aside. "*Take a seat,*" he gestured toward the chair opposite him. "*And close the door,*" he added quietly, the tone of the command softer, but insistent.

Tara sat, her eyes locked on his, trying to convey everything she felt without words—her concern, her frustration, her need for clarity. "*There's so much I need to say,*" she began, her voice heavy with emotion. She took a breath, grounding herself. "*First, I'm sorry. I'm sorry for accusing you of my parents' murder. When I saw them die, I lost all sense of reason. I believed what the assassin said without question. I didn't think. I didn't think at all.*" She dropped her gaze, a shadow of shame clouding her face. "*I'm ashamed of it.*"

Harshat, leaning back in his chair, let out a scoffing breath. "*Honestly, I would have done the same,*" he said with a knowing look. His words, though not overtly forgiving, held a strange understanding, a silent acknowledgment of the pain they both carried. But then, his expression shifted, and he leaned forward, his voice low and tinged with bitterness. "*But...*" he paused, his eyes darkening. "*He never treated me like a son. To him, I was just a tool, something to ensure the future of the kingdom. When neither of his queens could bear him an heir, he used a servant—a dasi—to do so. And then, when she threatened to tell the world the truth about me, he had her killed.*"

Tara's heart twisted as Harshat's grip tightened around her hands. "*That's why,*" he continued, his voice colder now, "*I don't feel sad. I don't feel angry that Kashi—or whoever did it—killed him. Honestly, I'm relieved. What I need to do now is clear Kashi of the accusation. She deserves to live peacefully, without the weight of this false crime on her shoulders.*"

Tara, though understanding the weight of Harshat's words, knew that even if they managed to save Kashi from the death sentence, it wouldn't bring her happiness. She would still remain the first wife of a king who had never truly loved her. The thought of Kashi's heartache, her sacrifice, weighed heavily on Tara's chest.

"*I'll get going,*" Tara said, standing up, her voice strained with the weight of their conversation. "*You have papers to work on.*"

Harshat gave her a nod of acknowledgment, and with one last lingering glance, Tara left his office. But her journey wasn't over yet—there was still one person she needed to see.

In the quiet of the prison, Kashi stood alone, her gaze distant. When Tara entered, she called out softly, "*Rani Kashi?*" Her voice was barely a whisper, as though any louder words might shatter the fragile atmosphere between them.

Kashi, dressed in the simplest outfit she had been given, turned toward Tara. There was a calm in her eyes, an acceptance that Tara couldn't comprehend. "*You're doing this intentionally, aren't you?*"

Tara's voice broke as she clutched the iron bars of Kashi's cell, her fingers trembling. "*Why would you say you killed the father king?*"

Kashi's expression remained steady, almost serene, but there was a depth in her eyes that Tara hadn't seen before. "*Trust me, this is my happiness,*" Kashi replied, her voice almost detached. "*I'm a coward, Tara. I've never stood up for the girls. I've let that guilt eat away at me. That's why I killed him. And I'm ready to face whatever comes next. Even if it's the death penalty.*"

Tara's heart shattered at the words, but she couldn't let Kashi go down this path. "*Don't talk nonsense!*" she shouted, her voice thick with urgency. "*Me and Harshat, we'll find a way to save you. Just wait for us!*"

But Kashi didn't respond with hope or denial. Instead, she stood, her hand resting gently over Tara's on the bars. "*I'm telling you this because I love you,*" she said, her voice quiet but resolute. "*Tara loves Harshat. And Harshat loves her too. But Tara would never accept his love out of guilt—guilt for breaking my heart. Even if she did accept him, I'm not strong enough to bear it. I can't take the heartbreak.*"

Tara's breath hitched, her mind racing. "*I won't let you do this,*" she cried, but Kashi smiled softly, the pain in her eyes unmistakable. She left, unable to say anything further.

"*Do you want your sister to live a life where she can never be near her love, just out of guilt?*"

Nayna, who had silently witnessed the exchange from the shadows, stepped forward, holding a letter in her hands. Her face was a mix of fury and confusion. "*Rani Kashi, what is the meaning of this?*" she demanded, her voice shaking with frustration. "*This letter—*"

Kashi's gaze softened, her voice gentle but firm. "*I can see the love they have for me, Nayna. I can see it clearly. That's why I'm doing this. But I won't let Tara live with that guilt, not when she deserves so much more.*"

Nayna's brows furrowed as she shouted, "*You're giving up your life for this?*" The words stung, the sharpness of her anger and confusion evident in her stance.

Kashi smiled a sad, bittersweet smile, her voice barely a whisper. "*Maine unhe apni puri zindagi de di, to jaan dene me kaisi jhijak.*" (I gave up my whole life to him, so what hesitation is there in giving my life away?)

Nayna left in silence, her heart heavy with the unspoken sorrow between them. The choice Kashi had made hung over her like a dark cloud, the finality of it weighing on her soul.

And then, the fateful day arrived.

Kashi, having been found guilty due to the lack of evidence, was condemned to die in the public square. The royal family had arranged for her escape, a path that would lead her to safety. But when they arrived to help her, they found her cold and lifeless, the victim of a sudden heart attack.

The news spread quickly through the palace, and in the days that followed, Kashi's absence was keenly felt by all who had known her. The halls, once filled with her quiet strength, now seemed empty. Tara and Harshat, though their love grew with time, could never forget the sacrifice Kashi had made.

Andrew, too, left his life as a mafia member behind, choosing instead to stand by Nayna as the queen of Nazabgar, supporting her as she ruled with strength and grace.

Time moved on, as it always does. But the memory of Kashi, of the love she had quietly given up, lingered in the hearts of those who had known her. Life went on, but it would never be the same.

Kashi's fate is to be described more in another timeline, in another memory.

The End

FAVORITE ANNOTATIONS

Write your favourite lines here and decorate them as you like

About

This is the first book of this series, meaning there will be other books connected to it. Many future characters are shown here as well as characters from this book will also appear in future ones. So if you're sad or not satisfied with your character, their role is not limited here. Stay tuned.

With love,
Rai (Tanushka Raha)